A Trail of Dreams

A Sasquatch Tale

Ursula Westfall

&

Rachel Westfall

CONTENTS

Prologue

A raven soared over the city, dancing around columns of dust, trash, and the occasional wayward leaf. She ducked through the market district, her wings sending clouds of flies spinning from their meals of decaying fish and withered root vegetables. The flies bit the exposed skin of the merchants, but did nothing to deter the wayward urchins who hung about in gangs, peeking from alleyways in hopes of snatching up discarded produce and other dubious treasures. Cackling, the raven curled around billboards and careened up neglected causeways to the city's edge, where factories belched foul smoke and the ragged ends of old freeways littered the landscape.

Finally free of the city's tattered boundaries, the raven calmed as she found a fresh wind to ride into the forest and up the river, through a motley collection of archaic villages. Before long, she sailed through Halftree Village, and she did not dream of the places she had travelled to get there.

Halftree Village was no place for factories, or gangs, or garbage. It was an intentional community, now three generations old, and its residents had chosen to follow the old ways of living.

Cheerfully, the raven stirred the blackflies and mosquitoes with broad sweeps of ebon wings until they chose to lie low, waiting for the air to still. She stirred the leaves on the aspen trees, making them rustle and whisper their secrets to any who would listen.

The raven cackled again with delight. This was turning out to be a very good day indeed.

* * *

The summer forest was a play of light and shadows in the early evening. The air was filled with the buzzing of insects, birdsong, and the chittering of squirrels. The cacophony was broken by the occasional huff or grunt of a larger forest creature, at which the birds and squirrels would momentarily fall silent before easing back into their eager chorus.

Higher in the mountains, stillness was easier to find amongst the cool, burbling streams and tireless stones. There were places in the mountains where humans had never walked. In those places, one could live out a life of solitude, undetected.

It was in those remote, silent places where the best secrets were kept.

But sometimes, even the most elusive of the forest's denizens were called to enter the perilous realm of human civilization.

What was the source of that call? Was it curiosity? Hunger? Loneliness?

In the case of one particularly hairy, smelly, and hapless young sasquatch, it was something much more surprising. It was friendship.

1. A gift and a dream

Estella sat on the edge of the porch, her legs swinging over the side, toes mapping spirals in the dust. Her hands were busy with thread and needle, and her eyes darted back and forth between her handiwork and the two smudge-faced toddlers playing in the dirt before her. Yet her mind was on neither task. It kept returning to the note that was safely tucked in her skirt pocket.

> *My dreams have grown dark. I'm following their trail to see what I can learn. Watch Erin for me, be my eyes and ears and I know she will thrive. I love you, sister of my heart. -Elena*

Elena must have left during the night, for when Estella had awoken this morning, Erin was tucked into bed between her and her own little girl, Emma. When she rose, she had found the note on the rough wooden table that sat sturdily in the corner of her cabin. The edges of the note were worried and slightly damp, as if Elena had rolled it between her fingers in indecision. The note was so like her: serious, focused.

Elena had been restless lately, withdrawn. Her typically cheerful, easy-going demeanour had given way to long silences, and there were often dark circles under her eyes. Elena and Estella were cousins, close in age. Born in Halftree Village, they were of the third generation to live here, and they were fully educated in the old ways of living. They had been pretty much inseparable since they were small children. Estella had always been the bold one, the risk-taker, and Elena had been a little more cautious, but quick to laugh and eager to join in many adventures. But since Elena's daughter Erin was born, the little girl thrived, while Elena seemed to retract into herself. The distance had grown between Elena and Erin's father, Ethan. Estella had worried that Ethan was behind Elena's unhappiness, but Elena had shrugged off any sympathy about that failing relationship as if it was nothing.

But *this*; this Estella hadn't anticipated. She realised now that she had been asking her friend the wrong questions.

You see, Elena was a dreamer. Of all the talents that had emerged in Halftree Village in the generations since their founders had left the city, hers was perhaps the most disconcerting. While anyone might worry about the future and the world around them, a dreamer caught glimpses and vague hints of things that were real, and things that were likely to come. A dreamer's anxiety was truly something to be concerned about.

5

Estella set down her sewing, stretched and walked over to gather up the children. Though her daughter Emma and Elena's Erin had been born just days apart, Erin was slight and frail in comparison, her complexion light and her hair a wispy, fair tangle. Her light eyes were slowly shifting to hazel. They were cast downward now, towards the patterns that her fingers traced in the dirt beside her.

Emma's full cheeks were caked in dust now, and she held a drool-smeared stone in her plump hand. Her huge brown eyes sought her mother's face trustingly, and the stone fell forgotten to the ground as she reached out with both hands, wanting to be picked up.

Grunting as she swung Emma onto her hip, Estella was glad that Erin was so slight. She picked the second girl up and balanced her on the other hip, both girls clinging to handfuls of her shirt with their grubby hands.

And so, with careful, practiced strides, she made her way through the village to find Nana.

* * *

It was nearing dawn as Saska approached the village. He didn't like to be around too many people. They made him feel anxious for some reason. He liked to let his thoughts run slowly, like a stream in late summer. Too often, humans pushed things along until everything raced and roared along with a spring-melt's vengeance. Remembering this, he settled himself in a thicket of

6

brambles. There were berries here. He sucked on a few ripe, squishy raspberries and licked the juice from his thumb, happily.

The sun still hadn't cracked the horizon when he heard the soft footsteps of someone approaching along the trail. Hopefully, he peeked out. *Estella?* he thought, tugging his lower lip anxiously. He hadn't seen her in weeks, and he missed her. In fact, it was the thought of Estella and her chubby daughter that had brought him so close to the village.

But the young woman who came into view wasn't Estella; it was her friend, Elena, and she was burdened with a backpack that betrayed her intentions to leave the village for days, if not longer. Puzzled, Saska ducked back behind the bushes and scratched himself with his blunt, dirt-ringed fingernails. Elena padded silently by his thicket, apparently unaware that she had an audience.

As the young woman disappeared from sight, a bushy red squirrel burst out of the bushes next to Saska, making the pointy leaves shake. He chattered excitedly, then scrambled up Saska's arm and climbed onto his large, domed head, grabbing fistfuls of fluff. Saska looked up at him questioningly with his heavy brow furrowed. The squirrel-- known affectionately as Twitchy-- continued to pull at his matted hair, digging through it as if he was looking for something.

The squirrel finally unearthed a small stone about the size of Saska's palm. He gripped the shiny stone between his teeth and clambered down Saska's arm hurriedly, then dropped the stone into his hairy hand and squatted nearby, chattering.

Saska examined the smooth black stone, turning it over. It was perfectly oval and it glistened in the morning sun like it had been polished, but there didn't appear to be anything precious about it. He shrugged, then tucked it back into his woolly mop of hair. It would make a nice gift for Estella the next time he saw her. Twitchy was finally quiet, though he was looking rather pleased with himself. Maybe he had hidden the stone in Saska's hair last night, while he was sleeping. The squirrel had accompanied him for the past two summers, coming and going as he pleased. He was annoying, but too small and stringy to be worth eating. Besides, Saska had grown rather accustomed to his company.

Under the watchful eye of Twitchy, Saska settled back down into the thicket and began collecting more berries. He reached for a huge, plump raspberry that was so ripe that it was already a deep shade of violet. Juice was dripping from it; the succulent berry would soon be infested with maggots. It would be a shame to leave something so delicious behind and let it go to waste. He pinched the berry between his forefinger and thumb, thinking it could be part of Estella's next gift. He paused, remembering how she'd reacted last time he'd given her a squishy berry. It had puzzled him that she had found it revolting, but he wanted to consider her feelings.

Maybe Emma would like it, Saska thought, smiling at the memory of the solid, cheerful little girl. He plucked the berry off the bush and curled his palm gently around it, then he rose and stretched with a grunt. Elena had been gone for several minutes now, and he hadn't heard or smelled anyone else in the area, so he was probably alone. Of course, he never could really predict where a human would be. They flitted around everywhere and rarely stopped to relax, like sparrows looking for a spot to nest.

He meandered over to a moss-covered log that had fallen alongside the trail, digging around in his hair until he fished out the shiny black stone. He placed his treasures on the rotting log, plopping the ripe berry on top of the stone. Estella usually had an uncanny way of knowing when he left her a gift, but he wasn't sure if she would be out this way today. She had her hands full with Emma lately, or with helping her grandmother in the village. She had been going on walks in the woods less and less often. He missed her; he ached inside. It was almost enough to bring him into the village for a visit, but not quite. There were simply too many people there for his liking, and some people were not friendly to his kind. Not friendly at all, he thought, shuddering with the memory of his encounter with a group of sasquatch hunters a few summers ago.

The sun peeked over the horizon, promising a glorious new day. The robins were singing, and the swallows had begun their daily acrobatics, scooping up countless winged insects as they wove through the gaps between the trees. Soon, humans would come along the trail to gather water or to bathe in the creek.

By the time the earliest risers wound their way up the trail, the sasquatch was gone. The only signs he left behind were a pair of large, bare footprints in a thicket of brambles, and a small gift of nature placed neatly on a log.

* * *

The forest was silent this early in the morning, the clouds ochre smears on the horizon. A sliver of orange light glimmered from behind the rolling hills. Even the birds hadn't begun their daily chatter when I set out from the village. I felt a pang of guilt at sneaking away like this, but I knew I had to go. I couldn't take the chance that anyone might talk me out of it. Worst of all, I couldn't bear to see Erin's face crinkle with tears as I said goodbye, so I left her sleeping. She would be fine in Estella's care, and I promised myself that I would be back soon.

My destination was not yet certain, as I wasn't sure what I was looking for, but each of my dreams had pointed to a threat of some sort that came from the direction of the city. It was as good a starting point as any.

I slunk down the leaf-strewn trail as quietly as possible, planning to find a way to get to the city once I reached the river. I wasn't sure yet whether I could walk along the riverbank, or whether I would need to build a raft. I had been high in the mountains many times, looking down over the valleys, so I had a rough idea of the lay of the land. I was pretty sure the river wound its way into the city. I had seen how it thinned to a silver rope beneath the black smudge that betrayed the city's existence on the edge of the sky.

Only Estella's sasquatch friend watched me go. I could smell him there, reeking behind some bushes, and I spotted his insane squirrel-friend twitching in a nearby tree. It seemed wrong to shatter the pre-dawn stillness, so I passed them wordlessly, respecting their privacy. Other than my two furry observers, the trail was empty of life.

Determined to get some distance between myself and the village, I pressed on. It would take me most of the morning to reach the riverbank, and I intended to be well down the river before nightfall. I could feel a thread connecting me to my little girl; strong, resilient. It hurt so much to leave her behind, but I knew our relationship would endure. This journey would not be safe for her. The city was a huge unknown, and the stories that had come out of there had been increasingly worrying. Women, girls, children, the poor, the landless, the homeless, the politically unsavvy: anyone and everyone could fall victim to the corporate entities that controlled the city's governance and crushed dissenters. It had gone beyond the problems of violence and banditry that had plagued earlier generations of city-dwellers. The city's problems seemed to be more entrenched now; the bandit lords and drug barons had been replaced by corporate managers who were just as quick to take advantage of the disempowered.

If my dreams hadn't been so dark and compelling, and if they hadn't worsened in recent months, nothing would have convinced me to visit the city. But the message grew louder and louder, until I heard it shouting in my head by day, not just in dreams, and my head rang from it. Something was very wrong, and the village was in grave danger.

11

I had warned the village elders. It had taken me weeks to summon up the courage to approach one of their impromptu councils. They weren't fearsome, but they could be intimidating without even trying. I thought about telling Nana in private, but I felt the matter was important enough to bring before the whole council.

The day that I approached their mid-day fire-pit circle, I had been feeling particularly upset by the dreams of the night before. Irritable and a bit sleep deprived, I interrupted their musings to tell them about the dreams, and about my sense of foreboding. I knew I had not been very tactful. Nobody responded at first. Then Nana sent me to fetch tea and snacks, discreetly dismissing me so they could discuss the issue in private.

When I returned with refreshments, Nana spoke with authority, reminding us that we couldn't take action if we didn't know the nature of the threat. When Nana spoke like that, blunt and clear, without a hint of question in her voice, heads nodded and the other elders grunted their assent.

I asked, tentatively, whether we could send someone out to find out what was going on. To my dismay, the council had decided that nobody could be spared; every pair of hands was needed in the village. It was summer, and there was too much work to do. Besides, the city was not a safe place to visit.

Leaving the council circle, I felt waves of anxiety rack through me. If anything, my sense of foreboding and urgency had grown worse. I couldn't sit idly and watch our doom come down upon us.

So here I was, slinking off down a shadowed trail with a few days' worth of food, without my daughter, and without the blessing of the elders.

I dearly hoped that I'd made the right choice.

2. The call

Estella helped Nana with her chores, and by mid-day, she was covered in sweat and grime. She was Nana's weaving apprentice, but Nana often had unrelated tasks around the house that she needed help with. Today, Nana had asked Estella to squeeze into the tight, cobwebbed crawlspace under her cabin and seal mouse holes with a paste made from pine-tree pitch and sawdust.

Nana sat on the porch watching Emma and Erin play in the sand beside her cabin, occasionally raising her voice to give orders to Estella, whose bare feet and dusty calves jutted out from beneath the wooden siding.

Estella slid out from under the porch and pushed herself upright. Emma toddled over, wrapping chubby arms around her neck and planting a hot, wet kiss on her cheek. Estella smiled and tousled the sturdy girl's hair, surreptitiously wiping her wet cheek with her sleeve. Erin was staring at the ground, enchanted, watching a troupe of carpenter ants march by. A thread of drool made its way from her lower lip towards the ground, unheeded. The little girl was fascinated with animals of all kinds.

Estella washed up quickly in a basin of rainwater while Nana brought out some basic fare for their lunch: homemade biscuits, nuts, and dried fruit. Estella's feet itched. She resisted the urge to scratch, instead sitting on a wooden stool and crossing her ankles.

"Do you need me this afternoon?" Estella desperately wanted to go bathe in the creek. Nana glanced quickly at her out of the corner of her eye, smiling slyly.

"Of course I need you. Do you think I can weave all these carpets on my own? You're not planning to disappear too now, are you?" The older woman chortled softly and popped a nut into her mouth. This was the first time she'd alluded to Elena's abrupt departure since Estella had brought her the news this morning. She didn't seem angry or even worried about it, though Elena had clearly gone off without the elders' assent.

"Of course not! Can I just go wash up in the creek? I'll come right back. I'm too dirty to do any weaving right now," Estella pleaded, trying to hold her voice steady. She wasn't sure why she felt so compelled to go to the creek right now, apart from being covered in grime, but the feeling had been growing stronger and stronger all morning.

"Of course," Nana retorted. "We can't have you handling cloth or thread like that!" She reached across and brushed a clump of dust and cobwebs from Estella's long, black hair. Estella's eyes widened; she hoped the cobweb had been abandoned before it had ended up in her hair. She suddenly felt very itchy all over. It was so hard not to scratch!

Estella stood and made for the door, then she paused and turned. "I can leave the girls with you, Nana?"

"Yes, yes, go on now," Nana replied, stooping to collect first one girl, then the other. She was surprisingly strong, considering how elderly and frail she looked. *Funny how she can pick up those two girls, but she can't get under the cabin to plug her own mouse holes,* Estella thought, cynically. She smiled to herself wryly as she hopped off the porch and began jogging through the village towards the creek trail.

Her sense of urgency didn't diminish as she hurried down the trail; if anything, it seemed to be growing stronger. *It must be the heat,* she thought. The day had really warmed up, and it would be so nice to get into that cool water.

As she approached her favourite bathing spot, her eye was drawn to a fallen log that lay beside the trail, covered in moss on its north side. A shiny black stone had been placed on the log. Atop it lay a rotten berry, like a signature. She grinned brightly, flicking the foul berry away then cupping the smooth stone in the palm of her hand. Her dear Saska must be in the area. She hadn't seen him in weeks, but his gift was unmistakable! Impulsively, she

16

drew the stone to her mouth and kissed it. Then, tucking it carefully into her pouch, she headed down to the water to bathe.

The water felt so good on her itchy skin and aching muscles! As she scrubbed the dirt and sweat from her arms, legs and face, her mind wandered. She heard nothing but the music of the creek and the occasional call of a distant raven. It was a perfect summer day. She decided on impulse to wash her hair, and then, because she couldn't weave for Nana while dripping wet, she perched on a flat rock beside the creek to drip-dry and catch some sun. She laid back, watching birds circle across a clear, blue sky, until her eyelids began to feel heavy. Lulled by the murmuring creek and fatigued from the morning's labours, she dozed off.

It seemed that only moments had passed when she was dragged back into consciousness by a rough-palmed hand brushing her cheek. She gasped in alarm as her eyes flew open.

* * *

The sun was high in the sky, and though Saska had stopped to eat from several berry bushes along the way, he was deep in the mountains when the call came. He felt a humming vibration in his head, insistent, pulling him back towards the village. What could it be? He tried to continue clambering up the rocky slope, but a sudden feeling of urgency nearly overwhelmed him. He stumbled and fell, sliding back down the slope. Scratching his head, puzzled, he realised he was going to have to go back.

Retracing his steps towards the village, Saska scrambled across the rocky landscape, worried and confused. He smashed through some underbrush until he finally broke free of the forest into a small meadow, ringed with willow thickets. A little creek burbled cheerfully through the meadow. The insistence of the call faded, turning to a dull throb inside his mind. Saska stood confused for a few seconds, then turned to leave. As he turned, something shiny glinted in the corner of his eye. He turned back, curious.

A small, black stone gleamed in the daylight between the leaves. It was balanced on the palm of a dark-haired woman's hand. *Estella!* Saska thought. She was holding the stone he had left for her earlier.

Estella lay on a flat rock beside the creek, unmoving, almost hidden from him by a clump of willows. As he approached her worriedly, he saw that her eyes were closed, and her expression was peaceful. But why was she just lying there? Was she sick? He squatted next to the rock and reached out to stroke her long, raven-black hair. His palm brushed her smooth cheek.

Her eyes fluttered open, her muscles tensing. Then she saw him and relaxed with a sigh.

"Saska?" she asked drowsily. "Why did you come here?" She stretched, then lifted herself off of the rock. She looked down at the black stone, as if just realising she had been clutching it while she slept, then tucked it into her pouch. A huge grin split Saska's face as he saw that she was unharmed, and he rushed to embrace her. She returned his embrace warmly.

"Why did you come here?" Estella asked again, her voice muffled as she buried her face in his hairy chest, but he just shook his shaggy head in reply. His strange experience didn't seem to matter anymore. They were together now; he was happy, and that was that.

* * *

As Estella disappeared down the trail, Nana made her way down to the communal fire pit with the two toddlers in tow. They meandered slowly, with detours for dandelions and butterflies, but they didn't have far to go. Before long, she was perched on one of the many stumps that ringed the fire pit. In the heat of the day, it contained only the blackened coals from last night's fire. She settled the toddlers down in a broad patch of sand, where they began to dig and play.

Two of the other village elders had arrived before her: Old Jack and Simon. They must have left some youngsters in charge of the fish camp today. She chuckled to herself. By the time you got to her age, anyone with fewer than six decades in their pouch was considered a youngster.

The three elders looked around at the sky, the fire pit, anywhere but each other. Nobody said so much as 'good day' until Myra hobbled over and perched on a log, wrapping her shawl tightly over her shoulders.

They were all gathered now, the last of the elders since Jessie had gone and died, shriveling up with some sort of lung disease last winter. Nana still wasn't used to him being gone. Sometimes she thought she could still hear his

19

scratchy voice, complaining about the diminishing size of the fish or the poor work ethic of the youngsters these days. He had always been the pessimist of the group, predicting harsh winters and droughts which rarely materialised. Yet, he had been the one who kept them all prepared in case the worst happened. Thanks to Jessie, the village had a full year's supply of dried food in storage, much of which was hidden in caches in the hills around the village in case they needed to evacuate.

Nana thought of Jessie now, wondering what he'd make of this situation. He was the only one of them who would have counselled action because of Elena's dreams, even if it was just to put a watch on the girl. Perhaps the rest of them were too relaxed, taking life as it came, never anticipating the worst.

And look where it had gotten them.

They had lost their dreamer.

Nana looked down at Elena's little girl, shaking her head. Elena had no idea what she was getting into. The city was a dangerous place, but even worse were some of the villages she'd run into along the way. Some of those people were very strange, backwards even. Elena was used to the safe, sheltered life of Halftree Village. She had no idea how differently others lived.

Of those who had gone away before, some had come back, shaken to the core. Others failed to return. Aside from concerns about the safety of those who left, the village itself was threatened by any exposure to the outside world. The less outsiders knew about Halftree Village, the better.

Myra cleared her throat and began to speak in a clear, low voice. Nana cocked her head to the side to listen.

The council session had begun.

* * *

Plagued by doubts and haunted by last night's dreams, I pushed my way through the forest. Though it didn't take long to reach the riverbank, I soon discovered that its shores were choked with brush, rocks, creek-mouths, and countless other obstacles. Though I was able to follow wildlife trails that meandered along the shore in many places, by mid-day, my arms were covered in scratches and welts, and I was plagued by swarms of hungry blackflies. It was time for what grandpa called "Plan B." Feeling determined, I sat on a boulder to eat a quick bite of lunch in the sun, then I set about building a raft.

There was plenty of dead-fall to choose from, and all I really needed were a few solid logs to strap together. They would need to be as long as I was tall, and dry so they would float well. I dragged a few good candidates together and sat back to size them up. I was suddenly grateful for my small, light build; the raft would carry me easily.

As I wove a length of rope between my raft-logs, securing them together, I thought of Erin and wondered if she missed me yet. Hopefully, she was so entertained by all the activity around her, she didn't even realise I was gone. I was thankful that she rarely nursed anymore; I breathed deeply and willed the thought away.

21

My raft ready, I selected a long piece of dead-fall to use as a push-pole, grabbed my pack, and pushed myself out into the river current. My plan was to stay close to the shore, so it would be easy to pull in for the night.

At first, this leg of the trip was uneventful. The river burbled along calmly here. The spring rush of snow-melt had passed weeks ago, and the river was well below its maximum depth. It was easy to let myself be lulled by the rocking of the small raft, the sun and sweet air, and the sight and sounds of swallows, dragonflies and the other insect-eaters darting above me. I laid back for a while, taking it all in.

Gradually, the river began to grow choppier. The sun disappeared, and I sat up, realising that the riverbank had grown steep, forcing the river into a narrow channel. As I picked up speed, I felt a stab of panic. There was a roaring sound coming from somewhere up ahead.

I desperately began poling, trying to push the raft closer to the shore, though the cliff-like riverbank was too steep to climb here. All my effort got me nowhere; the current held me tight. I breathed rapidly, looking around desperately for something—anything—to grab onto. The roaring sound was getting frighteningly close, and I could see no way to get out of the river.

Panicking, in moments I had reached the edge of a fall. It didn't look too far; the water dropped down in a few rushing steps that were perhaps twice my height altogether, or so I hoped. I grabbed onto the sides of the raft for dear life as I rounded the top of the fall.

With a couple of deep splashes, and a groan from the logs of the raft, I made my way over the fall. The raft dipped then quickly righted itself, spinning slowly in the water. Elated, I let go of the sides of the raft and looked around, grinning.

Suddenly I was in the water! The raft was gone. Where was it? I splashed around frantically, fighting the current. Then something struck me, hard. My vision faded to stars, and a puzzled thought skittered across my mind. Why could I still hear swallows?

* * *

The dream-world which found me then took me to the grassy banks of a very wide part of the river. The swallows swooped over the water, filling their bellies with countless small flies. Looking down, I saw that this dream was much like the others I've had lately. I was no longer wearing the sturdy clothes I had chosen for travel; instead, I was draped in the most grimy rags I had ever seen, torn and oil-stained but dry.

Something on the horizon loomed dark and ominous, a smudge beginning down-river, creeping through the sky towards me. My heart pounded; I could see the blood in my veins pumping hotly behind my eyes. This smudge was at the heart of each of my nightmares lately.

Hearing an odd gurgling sound, I looked back over the river. An ugly brown film coated the surface of the water, just barely visible, shimmering and opalescent. It seeped towards me as if drawn by my presence. I could see minnows darting in the shallows, their backs flashing rainbow lights, and as I watched, horrified, they stiffened as the slithery stuff oozed across them. A moment later, the fish rose and bobbed belly-up on the surface of the oily water, dead, and strands of tattered pale fish-skin swirled in the eddies. The reeds and sedge along the shore rotted under the contaminant's oily touch.

My dreams usually ended there, and I had spent countless hours replaying the scene in my mind, trying to understand the significance of each element of the dream. What did the dark cloud symbolize? What about my clothing, the oily river, the dying fish? Were these predictions of a certain future, or were they symbolic of something more obscure?

For the first time, instead of waking with my heart in my throat, I found my eye drawn to something new. A faint shape, something dark and massive, was gurgling up from the river's heart.

Bubbles sprouted on the water as a deep-blue, crested monstrosity rose leisurely from its depths. With a roar of water, a triangular-scaled leviathan loomed out of the river. Water cascaded down its sides in oily sheets. One by one, a series of thin membranes retracted from a circular dome on the side of the creature's head-- for surely it was a head, boldly crested and wedge-shaped-- revealing a single faceted eye of purest silver. My blood froze as the beast glared at me coldly from beneath the rocky shelf of its eye-ridge. I could only stare in shock as the immense serpentine creature studied me for a moment, as if gauging my worth, then abruptly shook its huge head in a spray of foaming white water.

With a slow blink, it drew the thin, curtained membranes back across that eerie silver eye.

The monstrous head slid silently back under the water, then it was gone.

As the dream faded, one question ran through my mind over and over:

What have they awakened now?

3. Hillbilly Falls

Rough slapping hands tore me from my dream. I fought and flailed, trying to throw off my assailant, without success. I was thrown down on my belly, hard. My lungs heaved as I coughed up rivulets of cold water. My hair clung to me in cold, wet strands, and I couldn't stop shuddering.

"Settle down, girl, quit thrashing around! I'm a-tryna help you here." A woman's elderly, quavering voice reached me through a series of hard thumps on the back. Who was attacking me? Was she trying to kill me?

As my coughing finally began to settle, I turned my head to look cautiously over my shoulder. A wizened face greeted me, atop a body strong and wiry as a bundle of old roots. "Who are you?" I managed to gasp. That set off another round of coughing.

The strange old woman chuckled, thumping my back again with a fist like iron. "I'm yer savior, that's what I am! Welcome, girl. Welcome to Hillbilly Falls!"

Hillbilly Falls? The name penetrated my misery and made me smile despite myself. She couldn't be serious. It was like something out of one of the old stories!

The woman was still nattering as I got my knees under me and tried carefully to stand up. "You can call me Maggie, girl. Whatsyername? Girl? I can't just be calling you girl, yasee?"

I shook my head, confused. What was she saying?

She gave me a look like I must be simple or something, then poked herself in the chest with a wiry finger, knuckles like the knots on a tree branch. "Maggie." She turned the finger towards me, and I watched it approach warily. It darted forward, jabbing me in the sternum hard enough to make me gasp, which set off another coughing fit. I leaned forward and Maggie grasped my shoulders, holding me as I hacked up another lungful of river water. Once the coughing finally eased, I breathed my name. "Elena. I'm Elena."

Maggie's face lit up with a grin; her mouth opened to show a red, pointed tongue and a full set of snaggly teeth. I pulled back, mildly alarmed.

"Old Maggie won't hurtcha, girl. Elena. Come, let's getcha up to da house. Getcha in front of a fire so you can get yerself all dried off. Then mebbe you

27

can do some carryin for me. Get some water and firewood, stuff like dat. Yeah, old Maggie could use a lil help around here. Even if this girl's missing a few bits and pieces up here." She tapped her forehead, shaking her head while tucking a covered basket under one arm. She nattered on as she hauled me along after her, those wiry fingers wrapped around my forearm like a vice.

"Wait," I said, "my bag!" Where were my things? Had they been lost when my raft went under? I wouldn't get far without food. I pried Maggie's fingers off my arm and stumbled back down to the riverbank.

Maggie stood imperiously, tapping her foot as I scoured the riverbank below the falls, looking for any sign of the rough fabric of my bag. No luck. I wondered how far it would have been carried downstream, and whether there was any point in looking for it. Discouraged, I rejoined Maggie, who looked down at me with an oddly pleased expression on her face, lips pursed.

"Well let's be going girl, daylight's a-burnin!" She sniffed and began to march energetically up the trail. I scrambled to catch up.

* * *

Estella meandered back to the village, happily; she felt warm and she tingled all over. Her nap had been lovely, but the reunion with Saska was ten times as good. He always made her feel so wonderful! He had let her bathe him in the creek, scrubbing his matted hair with handfuls of cleansing sand. Then he had leaned back against a rock and held her, rubbing her back and listening to her chatter on about life.

28

Whenever she saw Saska, he said little; his presence was comfort in itself. She loved to lean into his broad, furry chest and draw his arms around her, sitting in a sheltered spot amongst the bushes.

As she neared the village, she smelled the cook fires and heard the sounds of the evening communal meal. How could she have lost track of so much time? She shook her head to clear it, then started to jog. The whole village was there already, some gathered in small circles, others clumped around the large stew-pots which sat near the fire.

By the time she joined the fire pit circle, she was out of breath. Emma spotted her; the chubby little girl toddled over and happily clung onto her leg. Estella lifted her, smiling, giving her a huge hug and a kiss on the cheek. Emma grabbed fistfuls of Estella's blouse and hung on, legs wrapped securely around her waist.

Nana was perched nearby on a bench. She gave Estella a questioning look, then she patted the bench beside her. Estella joined her and opened her mouth to apologise, but Nana cut her off. "The girls are hungry. Better grab them some food, then get something for yourself."

Erin was playing in the sand at Nana's feet, and she seemed contented, but she sucked on the fingers of her left hand in a telltale fashion. Estella plunked Emma down beside Erin, then headed over to the cauldron to ladle up some bowls of stew. Emma toddled after her, grabbing her skirt and tagging along. Estella prepared three bowls: two small ones for the girls and a large one for herself; then she glanced back at Nana and added a fourth bowl for the older woman.

As she turned to go back to her seat, two bowls of hot stew gripped precariously in each hand, she nearly bumped into someone. Startled, she took a step back. It was Uncle John, a tall, broad man; Estella's nose was level with John's chest. She looked up into his face, holding the bowls steady. Emma still clung to her skirt. The little girl hummed to herself softly, swinging from side to side. Estella adjusted her stance so she wouldn't lose her balance, then smiled confidently up at John.

"You're back!" Estella was always happy to see her uncle; he spent weeks at a time living in the wilderness. It was unusual to see him join a large, communal meal.

John patted her cheek, fondly. "For now," he rumbled. More quietly, for her ears alone, he continued. "I hear your young friend has been in the area lately. I hope you warned him away." His brows knitted, worriedly. "It's not safe for him around the village."

Estella frowned, puzzled. Why had Saska come so close to the village? He hadn't been this close since those bounty hunters had tried to catch him. That was years ago! Since then, they had always met in the wilderness, a day or more away from the village.

Most of the villagers still thought sasquatches were only found in stories. John knew more than most; he was Nana's eldest son, but he was related to Saska, on his father's side. It was one of the village's best kept secrets.

John was big, and he was hairy. He was also half sasquatch.

"I'm not sure what happened, Uncle. If I see him again, I'll be sure to warn him to stay away." Estella pitched her voice low, matching her uncle's tone. Puzzled, she added: "Who told you? I didn't think anyone else would have seen him."

"Let's just say a certain squirrel alerted me to the situation." John's face creased with a lopsided smile. Saska's squirrel friend was certainly recognisable to anyone who had met him!

Estella sighed with relief. "Thanks, Uncle! We'll be more careful from now on for sure." John patted her cheek again, then turned to let her rejoin Nana on the bench.

Pensive, Estella distributed the bowls of stew. While the others ate, she chewed on the inside of her lip as her food cooled in her lap, forgotten. What had brought Saska so close to the village? She would have to ask him.

* * *

Saska tromped through the underbrush towards a clump of raspberry bushes, idly scratching his head in thought. He had finally left the creek after spending the afternoon with Estella; his stomach reminded him that it was dinnertime. He was still wondering why he had been drawn to the creek in the first place. That strange, insistent *pull* in his mind had brought him to Estella for some reason.

As he scratched his head, something squished beneath his fingers. He pinched the object between two grimy fingernails and pulled it from his scruffy scalp, revealing a partially crushed, squiggling louse. He popped it into his mouth, then slowly tromped over to a clump of bushes, sucking on his fingers. He settled down into the bushes; it was the same raspberry thicket he had crouched in that morning as he watched Elena leave the village.

His stomach growled impatiently as he plucked the plump, ripe raspberries from the bushes, stuffing them into his mouth two-handed. He swallowed hungrily, but as he reached for the bushes to gather more berries, he felt eyes on him.

Turning slowly, he swallowed as a prickle ran up his spine. At first, he saw nothing; then a squirrel, fur more matted and tangled than usual, burst out of the bushes and ran towards Saska. Twitchy was untypically silent, dark eyes wide with fear.

Saska lowered his hand and let the squirrel clamber up his arm. In moments, his bedraggled friend was perched on his head, scolding softly, almost inaudibly. Saska looked up at his friend, concerned.

"Did someone chase you?"

Twitchy's eyes were wide, black circles of fear in the little fellow's face, and he gripped Saska's hair in two tight, bushy handfuls. Intrigued, Saska looked back to where the squirrel had run from.

At first he saw nothing out of sorts. He rubbed his eyes; refocusing, he suddenly held himself as still as he could. Through the bushes on the other side of the trail, he spotted the glimmer of two huge, golden eyes. The pupils were slits. The eyes locked on his, unblinking, hypnotic. Saska did the first thing that came to him when he felt afraid. He squeezed his eyes shut and growled, low in his throat, then uttered a sharp, loud bark that rang in his ears. Twitchy's claws dug into his scalp painfully.

When Saska's eyes reopened, the lantern eyes of the beast were gone. The huge cat's back was to him now, and he watched as it slunk away between the bushes, tail swishing, leaving the faint smell of musk in its wake.

Saska felt a chill. He was used to being the biggest, scariest thing out there; it was rare that he encountered a more fearsome predator. Cougars brought out the most visceral fear in him. He nervously plucked a few last berries off of the gnarled bushes, then dashed away with the trembling squirrel still perched on his head, determined to get as far away from the thicket as possible.

4. A reluctant guest

Breathing heavily, I added a load of kindling to the rapidly growing pile and wiped the sweat from my forehead with my sleeve. As I heated up, the blackflies were drawn to me in clouds; I had been bitten in several uncomfortable places already.

Maggie had put me right to work as soon as we reached her ramshackle homestead. She lived in a rickety cabin, flanked by a chicken coop and a pig pen. The pig pen was empty, and looked as if it had been for quite some time, though several well-aged hams hung from the rafters of the cabin. A handful of sorry-looking chickens roamed loose throughout the clearing around the cabin, pecking at weeds and insects, clucking contentedly. There were no other dwellings in the vicinity of Maggie's cabin, though well-worn trails led off into the bush in every direction like the spokes of a wheel.

34

Hours had passed since our arrival, and the sun was low, casting long, slender shadows through the clearing. So far, I had hauled water, split and stacked wood, swept the cabin floor, and prepared a rudimentary meal of boiled corn grits drenched with some suspicious-looking gravy. Maggie hadn't let me out of her sight once yet. She puttered around in the cabin and perched on a wooden stool out on the lopsided porch, sewing and stuffing old chicken feathers into a threadbare mattress. The whole time, she eyed me warily through narrowed eyes. Our conversation had dried up quickly; she muttered to herself incessantly, and she barked orders at me from time to time, but there was no friendly banter between us.

What have I gotten myself into now? The thought ran through my head over and over, but I had no answers. I was used to forceful elders; resisting Nana was like trying to stop a boulder from rolling down a hill. Yet this woman made Nana seem like a wide-eyed child. Where Nana was warm and affectionate, Maggie was all hard edges, and there was a bitterness about her that skirted the edges of madness. She seemed like a woman who'd forgotten how to trust anyone. Or maybe it was just me; maybe she just didn't trust strangers.

If that was the case, though, why did she fish me out of the river and put me to work? It was truly a puzzle.

"Girl. Git over here." Maggie beckoned impatiently, rising from her chair and turning towards the door of the cabin. It hadn't taken her long to revert to calling me girl! It got under my skin just a little, but I didn't let her know of my irritation. I had the feeling that she'd only do it more if she knew it bothered me.

I entered the cabin behind her, and she pointed to a large, black cauldron. "Time to git some dinner stewing. We'll have a real feast. It's been forever since I had any company." She chuckled to herself, scratching her whiskered chin, eyeing me slant-wise. She set me to work filling the cauldron with water and setting it to boil on top of the squat, potbellied wood stove that dominated the centre of the cabin.

Maggie hobbled outside, then came back in with a triumphant chortle and an uprooted potato plant clenched in one fist, plump tubers dangling from its roots. She handed the bedraggled plant to me, gesturing to a cutting board and a large knife. I set to work washing, coring out the eyes and chopping the potatoes.

Balancing on her decrepit wooden stool, Maggie reached carefully up to the rafters with a long, hooked pole and brought down one of the hams, which was tied to the rafter with a red ribbon. She still muttered to herself, but I could only catch the occasional word. She seemed to be complaining about a man, but the cabin had only one small pallet for sleeping, and there was no sign of any resident besides Maggie herself. Grinning and chuckling, she grasped the ham and clambered off the stool so spryly, I began to wonder if I'd misjudged her age. She brought the ham over and plunked it on the counter beside the cutting board.

"Cut a slab off this, girl, and cube it for the stew. I've been savin' this here ham for a special occasion." She grinned, poking me lightly in the ribs with a bony finger. Her moods were as changeable as the weather!

I tossed the potatoes into the cauldron, then I tackled the ham. It was dry and stringy, and it challenged me to cut off an even slice. I hoped the stew water would soften it, or we'd surely choke to death trying to get it down. Maggie pranced and scuffled, muttered and grinned, adding pinches of dried herbs to the cauldron.

"You don't have pigs anymore?" I asked, curious about the ham, given the abandoned state of the pig pen.

"They ran off, they did. Jailbreak." She cackled wildly, delighted. "Smart animals, piggies. If we don't eat'em, they'll eat us. You watch out for dem piggies. They're still 'round here somewheres."

Suddenly her mood shifted; she flung open the cabin door and cast a paranoid glance off to each side of the cabin. A few clucking chickens edged across the porch towards the door; she nudged them out of the doorway with her foot and slammed the door. The chickens squawked in alarm. "They'll eat the chickens first, you'll see. Then they'll come for you and me." Her eyes rolled wildly.

Cackling again, she rubbed her hands together. "But not tonight! Tonight, it's you n' me, dinin' on that there ham." She pointed at the withered lump on the counter. "Tonight's our night to dine. And since I'm feeling generous, you

37

can take a bowl of that there stew up the hill to my husband. He can prob'ly smell it cooking already. He's prob'ly hungry too."

Husband? Hill? I was thoroughly confused now.

"Husband? Um, where does he live? Does he have his own cabin?" I kept my questions soft, not wanting to upset her mood.

"He lives in that cave up there on the hill." She waved towards the back of the cabin.

"He's been up there for three seasons now. He made me so mad, I had to give him the boot! But he's still my husband, so I share a bit of food with him now and again. Can't let the dried up old fart starve to death, you know!" If anything, she seemed even more pleased with herself. She rubbed her hands together vigorously, grinning sharply.

"Maybe the piggies will eat him in the end, like they did old Bill. Maybe I can catch some and make a fresh new batch of ham. Ham for my husband, husband ham. Mmm," Maggie muttered. I looked over at the bubbling stew in horror. *Husband ham?*

"Who was Bill?" I was almost afraid to ask, but I couldn't let it go now.

"My sister Nellie's old husband. She lives just over the way." Maggie gestured vaguely, unconcerned.

"He went out to feed the piggies one morning, and he never came back t' the house. Well, Nellie was right concerned that he'd run off or sumpin'. You just never know with men. So she grabbed her broom—for protection against wild hairy beasts and such, you know—and went lookin' for him."

"She didn't have to look too far, because the pig pen was open, and there was old Bill lyin' on the ground, and them pigs were chewin' away at him. The slop pail was spilled right there and everything."

"Nellie made a great big batch o'ham that night, slaughtered every last one o' them pigs. And that was it for pigs round here. It wasn't long after that when all my piggies ran off too."

"You watch for them piggies. They're smart, and they're still around here somewhere." That paranoid look was back on Maggie's face, wild and wary. She twitched towards the door, like she wanted to look out again.

"This ham… who made this ham?" I was almost afraid to ask.

Maggie looked at me sharply, then broke into a laugh. "Oh, don't you worry, girl. That ain't no husband ham there, that's my ham from the spring before. Don't you worry none. Nellie don't share her special ham with anyone. She's the jealous type." She chuckled and slapped her thigh, as if the idea was the funniest thing ever.

Sighing, I went to stir the pot. It actually did smell appetizing, despite the dubious ham. The pungent herbs made my mouth water.

When it was time to ladle out steaming bowls of the stew and settle down to eat, I made sure to put mostly potatoes and broth into my own bowl.

* * *

Estella rocked with the rhythm of the shuttle. The broad twine ran across the loom as the fabric grew quickly. As an apprentice, she still did basic work: blankets and rough fabric for making satchels and other utilitarian items. The finer work was still done by Nana, a master weaver. And slowly, Estella was being introduced to the secrets of the craft.

Not only were Nana's woven works beautiful, things were often concealed in the weaving, things which the village didn't want the outside world to know about. For years, Nana had woven works of art that kept veins of gold hidden from explorers and developers, making the land appear poor and the stone dull.

Other things could be brought to the forefront by a talented weaver. In a year when the fish were few, Nana wove a broad tapestry of blues and greens, swimming with the flash and glint of trout and salmon; that year saw a surprise run of fish late in the season. And in times of drought, a well-woven blanket would bring to mind the sights, sounds, and fresh aroma of the rain forest. A piece like that, made with skilled hands, could bring down the long-awaited rains, washing away months' worth of dry dust and bringing new life to the parched village gardens.

As Estella wove, she thought of Elena, wondering how far she'd made it on her journey. She hummed, throwing a loop or two of new colour into the weaving here and there, a small charm to keep her cousin safe.

She glanced across the room to Nana, who worked a larger loom to create a far more complex pattern. Estella knew that Nana's task was much like her own, though knowing Nana, she would work on a grander scale, keeping the whole village safe with her weaving. For all she knew, Nana would protect the countryside as well, if not the world as they knew it. Decades of practice had given Nana the skill and confidence to do it, though Nana was reluctant to admit to her own prowess.

The two little girls, Emma and Erin, sat in the middle of a huge basket of woven fabric, playing happily with a collection of little wooden animals. Erin's father, Ethan, had lovingly carved each one.

There was nothing like a bin of weaving to make the little ones feel safe, contented and warm. Their presence comforted Estella, and she smiled to herself as she slid the shuttle across her work.

Whatever happened, she intended to use every skill she had to keep her loved ones safe.

* * *

Saska hastened back into the shadows of the mountains, Twitchy lodged securely in his shoulder hair, the gleeful burble of a glacier-melt stream

41

accompanying him as he dashed between the trees. Branches slapped at his woolly face and legs as he sprinted, stinging and scratching, yet he continued to run. He felt a sharp stab of regret at bypassing deliciously ripe raspberries and other forest treats, but the strange creature he had seen near the village had put flight into his legs. He intended to get well away from the area before stopping to eat.

Eyes darting at every rustle of leaves or flicker of shadow, Saska allowed himself to relax when he realised that no animal pursued him. His shaggy frame damp with sweat, he heaved a sigh of relief and settled down in a clump of mushrooms, plucking one of them from the ground and holding it up for inspection. The colour was a very pale yellow, almost white, and the wonderful smell that wafted from it told him that it was at its prime. Maggots wriggled in and out of their little holes in the mushroom's stem, and he pulled these happily from their burrows, slipping them into his mouth and swallowing absently.

Off to one side, Twitchy scrambled up the trunk of a tree, then with a rustle of leaves suddenly burst back down in an explosion of fur and sound, chattering noisily. Saska looked over, then nearly dropped his mushroom as he saw what had caused the squirrel such alarm: another squirrel was in pursuit, only this one was much, much larger and *very* fast. Unlike his squirrel friend, this one was pure black and gleamed in the sunlight. The black squirrel was chattering almost as loudly as Twitchy. The newcomer chased Twitchy up the tree, then back down the other side, moving with the speed and determination of a predator.

Thoughts of predators made Saska shudder. He rose ponderously, popping the mushroom into his mouth, his teeth grinding the chewy flesh. Twitchy scampered over to him, squeaking, and scrambled up his leg to perch on his furry shoulder. The black squirrel stopped, glared at him, darted up a tree, then clung to one of the branches and began its scolding in earnest.

This was a variety of squirrel from another continent. An entrepreneur who found them "cute and lively" had imported them to the city and sold them to wealthy residents as garden pets. It hadn't taken them long to go feral, over-running city parks and chasing away the natural residents of the area. Now they were expanding their territory out into the wilds. But Saska knew none of this. All he knew was there were intruders in the forest, and intruders made him feel uneasy. When he felt uneasy, he started to get angry. He thought about grabbing the black squirrel and eating it.

Saska rumbled low in his throat, then barked a growl.

The black squirrel didn't run, but its ferocious scowl deepened considerably. Saska snatched at the squirrel with one massive, hairy hand, but the squirrel was faster; it darted higher up the tree and scolded him loudly. Annoyed and frustrated, Saska hunched his shoulders angrily and huffed away, heading back up into the mountains in a direction that would hopefully take him away from unwelcome company of all sorts.

5. Revivalists

It was growing dark by the time I headed up the path into the hills at Maggie's urging, a bowl of steaming stew balanced carefully between my hands. My belly was full, and to my surprise, I had found the dubious stew appetizing. The stew I carried now was for Maggie's mysterious estranged husband. She had given me abrupt instructions for where to place the bowl of stew before shooing me off the porch and slamming the cabin door, scattering a flock of startled chickens.

The rocky trail wove through some gnarled clumps of vegetation, climbing steadily higher. I watched for the landmark Maggie had mentioned: a large, flat stone like a table, set below a wide clearing beneath a cliff-face. I could only assume that her husband's cave was somewhere along the cliff.

I watched for any sign of pigs along the way, warily. Not that Maggie's paranoia had rubbed off on me; It just seemed like a bit of caution would be wise. But the woods were silent, and nothing stirred.

The moon rose, casting a glimmering light across the trail. The silvery glow shifted to orange as I emerged into the clearing. There was the flat stone that Maggie had described. It loomed in the light of the small campfire which had been lit at the centre of the clearing, encircled with large, rough stones. Near the fire sat a gaunt, heavily bearded man. He watched me steadily as I approached, the steaming bowl held out before me in both hands like an offering. He cocked his head to the side, his eyes narrowed. I handed him the bowl of stew, then retreated to the far side of the fire.

Silently, he began to eat. He didn't take his hard eyes off me.

I stood there, awkward; should just I go back down the hill? Was he going to say anything?

Uncomfortable, I decided to break the silence.

"I'm Elena," I said.

He nodded, chewing.

"Are you Maggie's husband?"

His eyes narrowed.

"She told me to bring you the stew."

He nodded again, slowly. Then he placed the half-empty bowl down on the log beside him. He wiped his mouth with a sleeve of his well-worn plaid shirt. A few drops of stew still clung to his beard wetly.

"Umm…" Darn, this was awkward. "So you live up here?"

He nodded again.

"Do the pigs give you any trouble?"

A bark of laughter erupted from the grizzled man. Startled, I jumped in alarm.

"There's no pigs around here no more," he rumbled, his voice rust and gravel. "Is that what the old bat told ya? She's right paranoid about them pigs." He grinned, and I let myself relax.

"What happened to the pigs?" I asked, wondering how much of Maggie's wild story was true.

"The last of'em got et, that's what. There's nothing left but a few shrivelled old hams down at the cabin. That's why everyone else packed up and got themselves outta here. Nothin to eat!" His expression was wry.

"Don't you believe nothin' the old bat says to you about violent cannibal pigs and such. She's gone and lost what's left of her senses. I just stick around in case she gets into some trouble and needs rescuin' or sumpin'."

Cannibal pigs?? I nodded, pensive. His story seemed to make sense, except for the cannibal part. Didn't that mean the pigs ate one another? Still, there were a lot of questions left unanswered.

"Where'd you come from anyway? I mean, originally? Are you and Maggie from the city?"

"We're revivalists, that's what!" He sprung up from his seat in excitement, sending the stew bowl flying. He scurried to snatch it up off the ground, keeping most of the remaining stew from spilling. He ran a callused finger around the rim of the bowl, then popped it into his mouth, tongue snaking out hungrily.

"Dinna she tell you? Us people, we set on an old culture to recreate. We aim to revive the old ways, learned from the songs and scriptures and hand-me-down stories. People used to survive like this, so here we are, doin' the best we can. It was fine til we ate up all them pigs…. I guess you should always hold a few back for breedin' and such, but folks got greedy. It was the ham competitions that done it."

Ham competitions? I raised an eyebrow at that.

"Them fools, they got all worked up about who could cure the best ham. It became quite a thing around here, ham this and ham that. Ham tossin' and ham boilin'. Ham fritters n' everything. They forgot all about survivin'." He shook his head, sadly.

47

"So the other survivors, they dragged their sorry asses back to the city, heads hangin'. Fools." He sat again, looking down at his bowl of stew, despondent.

"Maggie n' me, we decided to stay until our ham was all used up. Then she got readin' some stuff about tough hillbilly women from way back when." Scowling, he scratched his head.

"Apparently they was somethin' else, makin' do without help from nobody. She started gettin' ideas about men doing the women's work and such. Well I wasn't havin' none-a that. Men just don't do the cookin' and cleanin'; it's just not right. I told her, men do the men's work. Next thing I knew, she'd kicked me out."

"So here we are. Might hold on fer another season or two, then we're done."

"Where will you go?" I was shocked at the plight of this village. How could things have gone so wrong, in so many ways?

"To the city, I guess. Nowhere else to go." He looked like he was going to cry! Against all good sense, I felt my heart go out to him.

I took a deep breath, then let it out. "Not everyone eats ham, though. Couldn't you just eat other things?"

He looked up at me, expression shifting to stone.

"Think you're smart, eh? Where'd you come from anyway? You her new helpin' hand or sumpin'?"

I flinched, blinking. "Not at all. Just passing through."

"Well good," he rumbled. "Keep on passin' through. Don't let that old bat take 'vantage of you or nuthin'. Once she gets her claws inta you, that's it."

I nodded, thoughtfully. I had been thinking about moving on in the morning, but maybe I should just head out tonight. If only I had found my bag! I needed at least a few basic supplies.

When I left, the old man was staring into his fire, motionless. I was halfway back down the trail before I realised I had forgotten to ask his name.

* * *

Packing up her weaving for the night, Estella kissed Nana's forehead and tucked the blanket more securely around her lap. The older woman had fallen asleep in her most comfortable chair, and she snored softly. She was still tough as nails, but lately, her age was beginning to tell. Or maybe it was the added strain and worry of everything that had happened lately.

The two little girls had dozed off, too. They were curled in a warm, tangled heap in the bin of weaving, their faces rosy. Estella snuffed the candles before shifting Emma into her arms and carrying her down the dark village path to her own cabin. She tucked Emma into bed, and the girl groaned a little but didn't wake. Then she headed back out to collect Erin.

Though Erin was finely built, she seemed heavier while sleeping. Estella carefully leaned Erin's sleepy head against her chest, cradling her. Erin shifted slightly, settling in, but she didn't open her eyes.

Estella quietly shut the door to Nana's cabin, then turning, she jumped as Ethan appeared behind her on the porch. Erin's young, burly father always had a friendly smile for her. Tonight, though, he looked worried. He looked down on his sleeping daughter and gently brushed the fine hairs off her forehead with his palm.

Quietly, he asked Estella, "Where is Elena? Is it true that she's gone off somewhere?"

Estella nodded. She wasn't sure how much she should share with Ethan; she knew that Elena wouldn't want to drag him into this.

Ethan reached out for Erin and Estella carefully transferred the little girl into his arms. Erin nuzzled into her father's chest. She cracked an eye open, then seeing her father, settled back down to sleep with a tiny smile.

"I'll take her home tonight. Thanks for being so good to her. Can we talk about this in the morning?" Ethan was uncharacteristically solemn. He was typically a playful man with a pretty smile, popular with the children. His cheerful demeanour was a good counterbalance to Elena's serious, quiet nature. Until Elena's dreams began to haunt her, Ethan had always been able to make her laugh. It had been sad to watch them grow apart lately.

Estella nodded and said goodnight to the pair, then headed home to bed. But when she crawled under the covers, she found that she couldn't sleep. She wished she had Saska's woolly arms around her tonight; his mellow presence would soothe her anxiety. Restless, she got up and collected from the windowsill the smooth, black stone he'd given her just hours ago. She got back under the covers with the stone cradled in her warm hand.

She pressed her lips gently to the stone, thinking of Saska. She hoped he was warm.

Finally, sleep found her.

* * *

Saska lumbered along through the trees, picking his way through the forest and towards the scent of high-bush cranberries. Though the new crop wasn't in season yet, this was the perfect time of year to pick last year's deliciously over-ripe berries which clung to the branches here and there in ruby clusters.

The sun was setting, and he worked with haste to fill the empty pit in his stomach before it got too dark to forage. As darkness fell, he settled down in a clump of bushes and curled up. What with all the excitement during the day, sleep came easily.

Deep in the night, the strange mental call began again, urging him awake. It was insistent, buzzing and humming inside his head, pulling his thoughts in the direction of the village. He struggled to resist it, but he couldn't keep still. The call seemed even stronger than last time!

Scratching his head in confusion, he rose and began picking his way through the dark forest, back towards the village. Thoughts rushed through his mind like a roaring river. Would he be pulled to Estella again? Or was this something else? What was causing this feeling? Had something gone terribly wrong in the village? It was like an itch between his shoulder blades, right where he couldn't scratch!

He crashed through prickly bushes and over rocky slopes, the call in his mind painful now, throbbing like the sting of a hornet. It almost felt like something was chasing him to the village this time, instead of pulling him there. Why was that? *Is Estella sick? Has something terrible happened?* His thoughts worried him, and he ran even faster, anxious.

Bursting out of the forest onto the village trail, in the early pre-dawn light, he could make out the spiked shapes of the low roofs of village cabins. He had never been this close to the village before!

His mind rang with the memory of the warnings his grandfather had given him:

Stay away from the village! Humans will hurt you. Danger!

He tried to halt himself, but the call was pulling him along like a current. He slowed his stride a little and hunched his shoulders as he came into the village grounds.

He slunk carefully through the clearing between the cabins, sniffing the air. He smelled the scent of human, faint at first but very recognizable, a scent he'd always associated with danger until he'd befriended Estella. Instinctively, he looked to the right and glimpsed a shadowed figure huddled between two buildings. He knew he'd been seen by someone, but it was too late now to do anything about it. He was half tempted to find the person, clonk him over the head and drag him into the bushes before he roused everyone! The call was too insistent, though. He had to find Estella!

The figure didn't move, so Saska continued on, carefully picking his way between the cabins, wondering which one was Estella's. He was sure now that she was the source of the call. It felt like he was very close.

Raising his nose to the air and sniffing, he picked up a familiar scent. It was that delightful combination of milky baby and Estella's own warm, earthy smell, much milder than his own sharp odour. He had found her!

He crept onto the front porch of the cabin that smelled like Estella. The porch groaned beneath his weight, and a board or two crackled ominously. He hastened to the door and pushed on it. The door didn't budge.

How do humans work these things anyway?

Firmly gripping the door handle, he pushed harder. The door popped out of its hinges, and suddenly he was holding it up by the handle. He almost fell on his face when it gave way! Thankfully, he managed to catch himself, maintaining his grip on the door as well as his dignity. He shuffled inside and awkwardly leaned the door up against the frame. It didn't seem to want to go back in the way it had been before. He frowned, puzzled.

Then, turning, he spotted Estella in the dim light of the room. She was sound asleep, and Emma was tucked in beside her. The warmth radiated off them both.

Smiling, he shuffled over and reached out to brush Estella's hair off her face.

That was when the door flew in and crashed on the floor of the cabin. The room flooded with noise and torchlight.

* * *

It was just before dawn when Runt saw his first sasquatch.

Though it had been a sasquatch hunt that first brought him from the city to Halftree Village, he'd been living in the village for two years now, and the villagers had him convinced that sasquatches were imaginary.

After all, they had been living here for generations. If sasquatches really lived in the area, someone would have seen one by now.

He'd become used to seeing bears and even the occasional wild cat, usually high up in the mountains. But this? This was something else.

It was enough to send his heart into his throat. He was terrified!

Not daring to move, he stood between the outhouse and the cabin, watching the huge, hairy animal slink into the village with remarkable stealth. He tried to still his breath, sure the sharp gasps would alert the creature to his presence.

There was nobody around but him. Not even the roosters were awake at this early hour, calling up the sun.

A full bladder had roused him early from his bunk in the communal cabin he shared with three other young men near the edge of the village, where the trail led out into the woods towards the creek. Now a trickle of pee ran down the inside of his leg, unbidden.

He hoped he blended into the darkness as the monster's shaggy head turned his way. Maybe it worked, because the beast continued on into the village.

Questions flooded his mind.

What can I do? He didn't have a gun, a tranquilizer, a weapon of any kind.

What if that monster hurts someone?

What is it doing here? Is it after the chickens?

Did this happen every night, and he'd just been lucky not to bump into it so far? Or had some distant calamity driven the beast to desperate measures?

The monster was out of sight now, hidden behind the cabins. Hurriedly, Runt slunk into the outhouse to relieve himself, then he rushed back into the cabin.

Though he was tempted to dive back under his blankets and try to get back to sleep, he quickly vetoed that idea. That's what the old Runt would have done. He would *not* be a coward!

Hands shaking, he lit a lamp and began to rouse the others.

6. Eco-trolling

The people with the money seemed to have nothing to do but buy stuff, toss it over their shoulders, then race to be first to get the next model of whatever gadget was hot this week.

What was it going to take to bring it all crashing down?

Ferret had worked for the NottaBoss on this crew of eco-trolls for the past seven months. They'd been scavenging e-waste, boxing it up, and mailing it to corporate execs to try and get them to wake up. They'd pranked the production managers, top shareholders, and even the CEO of Green-Ware, the company that held this city in the palm of its hand. They had hacked the company's PR networks, sending out fake e-messages under the company name, spilling data on its environmental record.

It seemed like nobody was really listening.

The city was full of garbage, most people were scraping a living out of the trash, and the rich folks were content in their high-walled, sanitized, bullet-proof neighbourhoods. They'd donate a few dollars here and there to help starving children in some other country, so they could feel good about themselves while wiping their feet on the people who lived around them.

The NottaBoss had the team out collecting used toiletries today. He was cooking up something special to string up on the CEO of Green-Ware's car. Ferret wasn't sure what the end product would look like, but the work in progress which was spread out across the workroom floor looked promising. It was some sort of sculpture, molded from soiled toilet paper, tampons and other unsavoury used body products. A hood ornament?

Green-Ware had recently expanded its business into personal hygiene products, buying out several smaller companies.

At least NottaBoss still had a sense of humour about it all.

Before Ferret came to work on this team, he'd done all sorts of odd jobs. Debt collection, that was the worst of them. He hated working on thug crews, and when it meant roughing up grandmothers, it was enough to turn his stomach. Sasquatch hunting, that was one of the craziest crews he'd been on. They hadn't caught a sasquatch; they had been lucky to get out of the bush alive. He scratched his neck, remembering all those biting flies. He still had fine, white scars crisscrossing his wrists from the prickly thorn bushes.

The eco-troll crew was a much better fit for him. At least he didn't have to try and intimidate anyone in this job, and it felt good to put some pressure on the moneybags that ran this city.

Besides, he'd never been with a crew that laughed as much as this one.

Oddly enough, the crew members even seemed to *like* one another.

It felt weird not to get pushed around by his boss or his crew, but there it was.

Pulling a twist of toilet paper off an ugly brown smear in the alley, Ferret grinned to himself as he shoved the stinking relic into his sack. The trick was to grab the stuff before it rained. There was enough acid in the rain these days to eat away the paper, leaving sticky strands that weren't worth gathering.

Someone shuffled around the corner into the alley, hunched suspiciously, hood pulled low over his head. Ferret shot a quick glance towards the newcomer then made himself scarce, darting out of the back end of the alley. It wasn't safe to be caught alone here. Some people would rob you for your clothes, if you had nothing else worth taking. Spotting Carl between some abandoned, stripped vehicles, one street down, he jogged over. Carl had been on the team longer than Ferret, and he knew his way around. His bag of smelly forage was stuffed even higher than Ferret's.

Carl grinned at Ferret, a quick, sly greeting. He was a wiry young man with a smattering of freckles across the bridge of his long, thin nose. Ferret grinned up at the taller man, hoisting his sack of filth. Carl pulled a hard green apple out of his pocket and tossed it to Ferret, who snatched it out of the air and gave it a sniff. Surprised, he met Carl's eyes. "Where'd you get that?"

"Found a few in the park a couple streets down. Eat it. It's good for you."

Ferret bit down, his mouth puckering as the apple's sour juice hit his tongue. The only park he knew of around here was an empty lot that people used as a graveyard for their abandoned fridges and cars, though it might have been a real park, once. There were a few broken trees and grubby bushes here and there, fighting to reach the sun through the garbage and smog. It was astonishing that one of those trees had actually produced something edible! That's the sort of thing that you only expected in the wilderness, or in one of those walled communities where the rich people lived. He'd heard they could still grow a few things there, though pretty much everyone was used to eating factory food anyway.

For some reason, the taste of the apple reminded him of the wilderness. He'd eaten bush food there, a few times, when he was on that sasquatch hunting crew. He'd been wary at first, but the taste of real fish, berries and nuts had been surprisingly good. An odd sense of longing filled him.

Carl reached towards Ferret's face, and instinctively, Ferret ducked. "It's alright, you have a smudge there." Carl ran his thumb across Ferret's cheek, then held it up, triumphantly displaying a clump of soot. Ferret shook his head wryly. It wasn't like Carl had ever smacked him before, but old habits die hard.

"Thanks," he grinned, a bit sheepishly.

"Anytime!" Carl cocked his head to the side, his eyes sparkling. "I spotted a good stash of TP over that way. Let's go scoop it!"

Ferret jogged after Carl into the next alley, chewing slowly on the apple, relishing the tang of the sour juice. He ate it right down to the seeds, then pocketed them. It wouldn't hurt to stick those in the ground somewhere. At the least, they'd feed the rats, or even better, something might actually grow from them.

Light-hearted, he came up behind Carl and almost missed seeing the grubby, skinny girl who stepped abruptly out of the shadows into their path. Carl drew himself up short, and Ferret nearly ran into him from behind. The girl couldn't be more than twelve years old, but she had a fiery look to her, with her elfin features and knife-hacked hair. Ferret smiled, but his grin melted as the girl flipped open a long knife with a *snick* and waved it in Carl's face.

"Whatever you've got there, I want it. Drop it and back away." The girl's voice was hard and clear. Ferret knew that tone well; it was the sound of desperation. Nothing would make this one back down.

"No problem, but I'm pretty sure you don't want our stuff," Carl cajoled. He started to open the sack to show her. The girl wasn't amused; she waggled the knife threateningly and gestured sharply with her other hand towards the ground. Shrugging, Carl dropped his sack.

"The other one, too, or I'll hang you both up by your guts." The girl pointed maliciously at Ferret with the glittering knife. Ferret sighed, then tossed his bag down beside Carl's. The two boys backed slowly down the alley. The girl bent down to pick up the sacks, keeping her eye on them all the while. They took the opportunity to turn and dash out of the alley.

Ferret followed Carl at a fast run for several blocks before they stopped to lean against a wall, wheezing. As Carl caught his breath, he started to giggle. Ferret scowled at him, puzzled at first, but his laugh was infectious. Ferret grinned as Carl choked out the words, "The t-treasure, j-just wait til her gang sees what she scored, all that d-dirty t-toilet paper! Hee hee hee, she'll never hear the end of this one!"

Chuckling and shaking his head, Ferret led Carl by the arm back towards the crew's meeting-place. Their scavenging was done for the day, and though they had nothing to show for it, Ferret's steps felt lighter than they had in years.

* * *

I wound my way down the trail to Maggie's hut. It was a clear, cool night, and the moon was high, stars glittering in the darker corners of the sky.

Before long, the knotted, scruffy pines and spruces parted. Maggie's clearing opened before me, and there she was, sitting in an old wooden rocking chair on the porch, snoring loudly with her wiry-haired chin tucked down against her bony chest. Her broom lay across her lap, its handle clutched loosely in her withered fingers. I imagined she must have fallen asleep while guarding her cabin against an onslaught of vicious pigs.

Silently, I approached, not wanting to disturb her sleep. I thought I would collect a few necessities, then head off down the river. The dregs of this odd community had disturbed me, and I didn't feel comfortable remaining here any longer.

I stepped carefully onto the porch, wary of the warped, creaky floorboards. Fumbling for the doorknob, I glanced over at Maggie; her basket lay beside her chair, a jumble of filthy rags spilling over its sides. My breath caught as I recognized the slim strap of my bag hanging over the side of the basket.

She has my things!

With a flash of anger, I forgot all caution and strode over to snatch up my bag. Maggie woke with a start, her face contorting as she shrieked and swung the broom at me.

"You old thief!" I yelled, darting off the porch with my bag. Maggie hadn't stopped hollering and swinging her broom; she had risen from her chair, but she seemed reluctant to leave the porch. I ran for the trail that led back to the river, its stony track gleaming in the moonlight.

I ran for quite some time, weaving between the stunted trees. Once I was certain that I wasn't being followed, I slowed to a walk. The trail wended its way along the river, downstream. My pulse gradually slowed, and my anger cooled. Eventually, in a small grassy clearing beside the softly burbling river and its clear rushing waters, I settled down to catch a few hours of sleep, my head resting gratefully on my hard-earned bag. It was lumpy, but that pleased me, as it meant it probably still contained its original contents.

The hypothetical problem of the feral pigs hadn't even crossed my mind.

You can imagine, then, my surprise when I was awakened before dawn by the sound of enthusiastic snuffling.

7. Wild encounters

Starting at the noise, not to mention the damp thing sliding across my chest, my eyes opened to meet a pair of beady, jet-black eyes set in a sunken face. The thing waggling across my wiry torso was the snout of this sepia-furred, hulking beast that stood with legs splayed, nearly straddling my stomach. How I slept through the arrival of the pig, I have no idea. Either way, the creature was leaning down into the folds of my sturdy travel garb, snuffling cheerfully.

Moonlight weakly illuminated the beast's tusks and glittering eyes. I wouldn't have been able to see the stiff pillars of the boar's legs flanking my chest without the gift of that moonlight. His wiggling rolls of fat had begun to sag down onto my stomach; I was trapped beneath his paunch.

The rank, musky stench of the beast's body odour and grimy pelt was reminiscent of Saska's. The thought of the sasquatch looming over me in the night, as if to kiss me yet crushing me under his bulk, made me snort with amusement. Saska and I were friends, certainly, but the idea of a sasquatch falling in love with me was ridiculous in this context. Besides, the boar's stiff whiskers were tickling my neck.

At the sound of my snort, the boar hesitated, cocking his head. He looked so comical, I coughed out a short laugh. With the slapping of a paunch against my stomach and the rubbing of coarse fur against my neck, the creature stumbled backwards a step or two. Shaking that great head of his, he waddled off into the night's embrace, leaving nothing behind but a hint of his bestial stench. A rustling of the undergrowth, then the animal was gone.

With the boar's departure, my humour quickly evaporated. Though the sky was still inky black and there wasn't even a hint of the sun on the horizon yet, my stomach growled and churned. My high metabolism had set to work; I hoped the river water hadn't spoiled my stash of food, and that Maggie hadn't taken anything from my bag.

Warily watching the forest for intruders, I got to my feet and opened my bag, encouraged to find that my stash of flat-bread was intact and undamaged. I squatted to chew on a wedge of the dry, grainy bread. Brushing the crumbs from my tunic, I wondered idly where the pig had originated from as I settled down and rested my head on my bag once more.

Later, I woke to an extraordinary magenta sunrise, the back of my head throbbing from sleeping on my lumpy bag. The clouds were wispy amber streaks on the horizon, promising a calm day. I opened my bag and glared sourly at my stock of flat-bread—all that was left of my food stockpile. It seemed Maggie had helped herself to my dried fruit and nuts. Snarling in frustration at my pitiful food-stash, I decided it would have to do for now. I could always forage for nuts and berries along the way.

I nibbled at the flat-bread with only a flock of waxwings for company. The birds paid me little attention as they sang to the dawn from their spruce perches. As I rose to rejoin the river trail, the birds shrieked a warning and scattered in a flare of crimson and russet.

After the waxwings, there was little in the way of wildlife as I made my way along the river. I occasionally caught a flash of something brown from the corners of my vision, and on a few occasions, I heard something crash away through the bushes. I avoided the startled beasts, and it seemed they were intent on avoiding me, too.

The landscape began to grow more arid over the course of the day. Eventually, it was almost desert-like with massive, sandy hills and scrub-like underbrush. There were some ancient, rickety wood enclosures and discarded farming tools scattered haphazardly across the sand, yet the notion of farming in such an impractical location seemed absurd. Trees, some sort of oak, used to grow here, but now they were gnarled, bowed and long-dead. I was amazed at just how much the landscape could change in a day's travels. Yet, the river continued to wind on through the lifeless soil.

Despite the ruin of this land, the flashes of wildlife grew more common. They continued to avoid me, but dust was kicked up in their wakes, and I spotted steaming piles of pellet-like droppings.

I settled down in the lee of a sand dune, scraggy bushes clinging to its peak. I was feeling decidedly exhausted, and I was covered with reddish dust. I removed another slab of grainy flat-bread from my pack and began to chomp on it. Just as I bit down, I was startled by another flash of pale brown which darted past me. My portion of flat-bread, tasting unsurprisingly stale and monotonous by then, nearly fell from my hand.

Another beast, coarse-furred and extraordinarily mischievous-looking, lumbered across my line of sight beside the riverbank. Finally, I was able to take a proper look. It was some sort of mottled pig, and it plodded along the river, apparently unaware of my presence. This was no feral domestic pig; it was something else entirely. The hillbillies were crazy if they'd sought to tame these beasts. More likely, this was neither a wild nor a domesticated pig, but some sort of hybrid. This creature bore a heavy, tousled pelt entangled with sand and the mangled, desiccated twigs of oaks. She was enormously fat, and was moving so inelegantly she was nearly limping, and her snout was twisted in a perpetual smirk. I wondered what the pigs were eating to be so well-fed, given the barren environment they were living in.

Once the huge pig had meandered out of sight, I allowed myself to finally release a breath, retrieving my flat-bread from my lap and scowling as I noticed that it was dusted with orange sand. Pulling my bag to my side, I finished my flat-bread then settled down to camp for the night, eyeing the riverbank warily for pigs. Other than hoof marks ground into the dust and the small olive pellets that were their droppings, there was no sign of them that night.

I sat pensively as the sun sank into the west, shockingly scarlet, and the stars slowly emerged, glittering. As night descended upon this desert-like terrain, the craggy mounds of sand looming above me became oddly sinister. The twisted shapes of the dead oaks created looming silhouettes which made me think of the claws of a great cat.

The moon rose, a golden globe that dispelled the strange shadows and lessened my worry about the pigs. When I finally laid down to sleep and cushioned my head with my pack, the only thing I could think about was home. Things were so calm there, so normal. I couldn't wait to get back to the serenity of life in the village.

* * *

Saska rolled over with a grunt as the wooden door crashed to the floor, raising a cloud of dust. Emma woke with a series of punctuating coughs, the type that preceded a good, loud scream. Estella quickly hushed the child, bundling her into her arms as Saska loomed towards the doorway, squinting down through the flare of torch-light. Alarmed, Estella called out, "Who is it?"

"Sorry, girl," came John's rumbled reply. "The door was loose."

Sighing in relief, Estella smiled in the direction of her uncle's voice. Her eyes were crusted with sleep, and she still hadn't adjusted to the light.

"What's this big galoot doing in here?" John's voice had risen nearly an octave, strained with worry. "I thought the two of you knew better!"

Saska hunched his shoulders worriedly, scuffing one bare, furred foot in the dust that had resettled across the floor.

"Half the village has been roused. That new kid spotted you, you big hairy lump, and he thought you were going to eat us all! He's roused everyone," He chuckled wryly. "Oh well, the younglings were gonna find out sooner or later."

Several faces appeared, pale as moons, peering around John's broad back.

"A sasquatch!" one of the boys bellowed, rushing into the cabin over the fallen door. A lantern bounced in his hand, casting random beams of light around the room. Blinded by a golden ray from the lantern, Saska yowled, reeling back and flinching into a ball with his hands flung over his eyes. At this roar of pain, a cacophony exploded in the cabin as two more young men burst in, lanterns in hand. Saska shrank into the corner beside the bed, eyes stinging.

"Go back to bed, y'all. It's just Estella's boyfriend, come visiting. Go on, back to bed!" John attempted to shoo them away with the backs of his hands, and the onlookers slowly backed out of the cabin and off the porch. They muttered to one another, glaring back at the cabin door warily. John stepped off the porch and began herding them away from the cabin.

Just then, Runt appeared, torch in hand, another gaggle of youths trailing behind him. He rushed past John and burst into the cabin. By then, Saska had risen and was approaching the door. Runt halted abruptly, his nose a fingers-width away from Saska's woolly chest, eyes wide as saucers. Drawing in his breath for a scream, he instead sucked in a lungful of dust, and his fearsome bellow came out more like a strangled cough. Eyes watering, he spun away, panicked. Saska grabbed his shirt collar between his thumb and forefinger and held on, lifting Runt onto the balls of his feet. He turned to give Estella a puzzled look.

"Better put him down," she chided. "He's scared half to death!"

Saska let go, then attempted to retreat behind Estella, who now held the sleepy Emma clutched in her arms. At least Emma hadn't started screaming. Saska felt he'd had more than enough social stimulation for … well, for one lifetime!

Plenty of people surrounded the cabin now, and it didn't take long for the youngsters to storm into the room, tossing it into a shapeless mass of confusion. Saska could hear Estella's startled yelp as she was thrust aside, then several young men gathered around him and began poking at him curiously.

Now, this injustice provoked a reaction from him. Rising and looming over the nosy humans, he threw his fists outwards, battering aside two youths who had been poking him in the belly. Caught off-guard, the youths fell firmly onto their behinds, knocking two others to the floor behind them. These new obstacles, fortunately, made the seething mob hesitate. The only one left standing inside the cabin was Runt. He slowly looked up to meet Saska's eyes, then he tentatively lifted his torch.

Though Runt's action sent a painful stream of bronze light into Saska's eyes, he forced himself not to recoil, his hands clenched into fists at his sides. He raised one massive fist, preparing to strike the young man, bringing his torment to an end. Estella halted him, a hand firmly on his arm. She had thankfully recovered herself enough to make her way back to his side.

"Quiet, everyone!" Estella snapped over the clamour as the fallen youths climbed uneasily to their feet, wincing and rubbing their backsides. The words Estella snarled were surprisingly harsh, enough to make everyone freeze. "He's my boyfriend," she continued, more softly. "Can't anyone walk around the village in peace anymore?"

"But I thought it was... it... that…." Runt trailed off, then pointed an accusing finger at Saska, who stood dumbfounded.

"You are, aren't you? A sasquatch! Like that scientist Longnose Knobbly-knees or whatshisname was after!"

His mind took it all one step further, and he realised... *That little girl must be half sasquatch!* He goggled stupidly at Emma who sat snugly on her mother's hip, sucking on one hand. She looked human enough!

John stepped back into the cabin and set about removing the five agitated young men. The boys who had been knocked down left quickly enough, but Runt hesitated in the doorway.

John put an arm around Runt's shoulders and walked him out of the cabin. "Come along, then. We had better go talk." The smooth rumble of his voice seemed to calm the frightened younger man, though Runt was still looking rather red in the face.

As their backs disappeared from the porch, Estella peered out, eyeing the remaining youngsters who were clustered about the cabin like a flock of chickens at feeding time. "Go on then," she chided. "You heard what John said. Back to bed." Finally, the last of the stragglers wandered off.

Plopping Emma down firmly on the bed, Estella turned to lift the heavy wooden door from the floor. She propped it precariously across the door-frame. She sighed. It wasn't perfect, but at least it gave them some semblance of privacy.

Turning back to Saska, she found him sitting on the bed beside Emma. His large, woolly head hung sadly.

"What brought you here?" she asked, softly. He was reticent at first, but slowly, patiently, she managed to coax the story out of him.

A compelling urge to join her? Not once, but twice? Whatever could have made this happen?

Emma, reluctant to return to sleep after all the excitement, sat on the bed, her plump legs crossed, playing with the smooth stone which Saska had given to Estella. She had found it tucked under her mama's pillow, and right now, the adults were too preoccupied to notice that she had it. Curious, she brought it up to her mouth and tasted it. The taste was dusty, metallic, good and cold.

At that moment, Saska sat bolt upright. His eyes grew wide.

"What is it?" Estella asked, confused.

"Emma!" Saska said, "Must see Emma!"

The little girl peeked around her mama's back, into her papa's dear, furry face. Worry lines creased his forehead. They looked funny. She reached out to him, giggling. The slobbery rock forgotten, she let it fall.

Estella's hand shot out, catching the stone before it hit the bedding. With a look of wonder, she met Saska's gaze. He put his broad hand over hers, encasing both her hand and the gleaming, black stone. With his other hand, he brushed back Emma's fine, black hair.

"I think I'd better bury this stone somewhere safe," Estella breathed, voice shaky. "I don't know what it is, but I think it could get us into a lot of trouble." Saska just nodded, slowly. He wasn't sure what was going on, but he trusted Estella.

Together, they pried a stone from the cabin hearth, dug a little hollow in the mortar to cradle the special rock, then tucked the hearthstone back in its place.

On the bed sat Emma, watching all the while, rocking and humming to herself.

8. A broken world

I was roused the next morning by a stream of hazy light and the eager chuckling of the river as it flowed on towards the city. My hunger gnawing at me and my mind filled with urgency, I scrambled upright, shouldering my ominously thin pack. Not pausing to eat, I began to trek alongside the river towards the city, pursued by fragmented memories of a haunted dream. As I walked through the rising dust, I was sure that I felt the sunken eyes of pigs boring into my back. I spotted an occasional flash of umber darting away from my path.

In the dream I had just awoken from-- no, it was a *nightmare*-- I was standing deep in the forest that surrounds Halftree Village. The rich scents of loam and peat wafted over me, and I was surrounded by stately old pines which were robed in lichen. The calls of birds and the occasional chatter of a squirrel filled the air. I let myself be immersed in the serenity of the forest, the drooping branches surrounding me in a lush embrace. As I admired the familiar landscape, no impressions of urgency or fear assailed me after months of strain.

The mood of the dream abruptly changed as roiling blackness like foul smoke spilled between the trees, rupturing my sense of peace. Helpless to do anything but witness with horror, I watched the ancient trees around me blacken and wither, millennia compacted into moments as if the pollution had the force of a fire. The ambient cries of wildlife trailed off and vanished as my vision was clouded in filthy smog. My senses recoiled from the foul reek of burning black oil. Then, after what seemed centuries of torment compressed into mere moments, I could sense nothing, nothing at all. Even the smog disappeared, for there was nothing left to fuel the fires and they were defeated by their own brutal, ravenous hunger.

The fractured vision plagued me for the entire course of the day as I plodded wearily across the rolling dunes of sand. About an hour into my journey, I was granted a glimmer of hope. Though the landscape remained arid and cluttered with the ancient remnants of farms, the porcine flares of pink and tan in the corners of my eyes were growing sporadic. Maybe I was finally leaving the pigs behind!

Once the sun was high in the sky, the grating of my empty stomach had mounted to a furious hunger. The hog droppings and hoof-prints had disappeared from the riverbank completely, so I figured it would be safe to stop for a bite to eat. The terrain was slowly becoming more level and fertile, and the litter of unsuccessful farms had been replaced by a few scattered settlements which looked inhabited. The land had been cleared for agriculture. I avoided the cottages with their tidy gardens and quaint stone walls, not wanting a repeat of my experience with Maggie.

After a short stop for lunch, I continued to hike through the farmland, following the river. The water did not burble gleefully as it had further upstream. Instead, it moved with the deliberate sluggishness of a channel laden with silt and ash. The sky was also tainted with a dull, smoke-smeared veil. That fouled atmosphere was unmistakable; I was nearing the city. For good or ill, I would reach it by the evening.

As I continued on, signs of the city became more evident. The quaint farms were replaced by metal-fenced industrial lots and decrepit factories, and the landscape was dominated by weeds and broken strips of asphalt. The river crawled like a beast drawing its last breath, oil glittering in oozing currents across the surface of the grey water. Sluice pipes emerged from the riverbank here and there, belching revolting filth which slunk in foul eddies through the water.

The flavour of the air worsened, thickening with exhaust, chemicals and smoke. Unused to breathing such dirty air, I found myself gasping raggedly for every breath. The soil beneath my feet grew increasingly barren until it resembled the sand in the desert-like region I had passed through earlier in the day. Garbage fluttered by me.

As I neared the city itself, night fell like a shroud across the infertile land. The quality of light had been reduced to an ugly haze, smeared with the artificial lighting of the city. I stumbled blindly towards the source of that light, occasionally tripping over rubbish or dislodging something horridly damp and squishy with my feet.

Greasy orange pinpricks of light showed me where the city lay. I barely noticed the disappearance of the river as my path diverged from it. Before long, I entered the outskirts of the city and its smeared penumbra. This part of the city was nothing like the opulent neighbourhoods that I'd heard about. The houses were squat and caked in filth, and I could smell rotting garbage. I wondered if anyone would let me spend the night in their home. I could hear drunken retching from down one of the gloomy alleyways, followed by a disturbing chortled laugh. I realised I was probably on my own for the night, as I would not go anywhere near the source of those noises.

Feeling grimy and drenched with sweat, I sank down into a crevice between two homes. A soft rustling noise came from the foundation of one of the crudely-built houses; it might have been a mouse or a rat. Despite my feelings of unease, I slumped rapidly into a deep sleep.

* * *

It was with some hesitance that Ethan knocked on Estella's door shortly after dawn. The night before had been disrupted; the whole village had awakened after Saska made his unprecedented visit. Ethan wasn't sure how warmly Estella would welcome him, under the circumstances.

But this, he decided, was important.

He was worried about Elena, and it was high time someone went after her. Nobody else seemed to be volunteering, so that someone was him.

He rapped on the door gently, as it was lodged against the door frame but its hinges hung free. Erin clung to his jacket, legs wrapped around his waist like a little monkey. She blinked groggily.

He heard movement from inside the cabin, though it was several minutes before an equally groggy Estella slid the door aside.

"Can you watch Erin for a few days? Or maybe a bit longer? Elena needs my help."

"What?" Estella scratched her tousled head sleepily. "You heard from her?"

He shook his head. "Just a feeling. I'm going after her."

Estella looked cynical. "She might not like that much."

"She never knows when to ask for help. She needs me, and I'm going after her." His voice began to rise in agitation.

"Well, good luck with that. Sure, I'm always happy to have the little one here." Estella reached over for Erin, who happily swung over into her arms. Still shaking her head, she watched Ethan march off, his stride full of determination.

"Be careful!" Estella called out after Ethan, and he waved at her dismissively over one shoulder.

Estella turned back into the house and tucked the groggy little girl into her bed beside Emma. Erin promptly nestled in and went back to sleep as Estella quietly slid the door back into place across the door frame. She'd have to see if someone could help her fix that today. Later.

It had been a long night, and neither she nor Saska had slept after all the ruckus died down. Saska had slipped away into the forest, unwitnessed by anyone but Estella, in the gloaming pre-dawn light. Now that the strange call-stone was safely buried in the hearth, she didn't anticipate a repeat of last night's chaos.

Hopefully Uncle John had been able to get the young men to settle down. The last thing the village needed was some more sasquatch hunting drama. The village had its secrets, and it was best they were kept that way.

Sighing, she slid back under her covers and wrapped an arm around the two warm, sleeping girls. Hopefully they would sleep in, so Estella could do the same.

9. An old friend

I awoke with a groan, my eyes adjusting poorly to the diffused sunlight which streamed between the houses. I could hear malicious cackling, followed by the sound of bare feet pattering across asphalt and muttered whispers.

"Lookit, she's wakin' up!"

"Throw a shoe at her or sumpin', then!"

An inelegant whine, "But we need dem shoes, T.E.E.! We needum!"

"We could always sell 'em," a reedy voice offered with a hysterical giggle.

However, this was countered in a grating voice by, "T'her, Trashbag? This from you? You can't even throw straight, can't ya! This is what it's all about!" A dramatic pause, then, "Lookit him, don't ya! He can't even throw straight--"

The voice was abruptly cut off, followed by a squealed, "I told ya so! Lookit, she's wakin' up!"

I flung myself from the hollow where I had been huddled in the crook of the alley, squinting in the dingy light. I found myself snarling down at a band of five battered-looking urchins, clothed in tattered t-shirts and faded jeans the colour of mud. Their skins were so coated in grime it was hard to tell where the clothing ended and where the child began. Wide, innocent eyes stared up at me from their smeared, grubby faces.

What was quite obviously *my* bag dangled from the narrow shoulder of one of the youths, and from another shoulder, *my* shoes, suspended by their laces. It was only then that I noticed that my feet were as bare as those of the urchins.

"Give me my stuff back. *Now,*" I found myself grinding out, struggling to contain my rage.

At that statement, the alleyway, little more than a dirtied nook, burst into chaos.

"Here, take these shoes! Hand-woven! Only fifty dollars!" one of the scrawny youths shrieked, attempting to thrust the footwear towards me. His witless grin revealed yellowed teeth.

Another urchin, presumably T.E.E. from his rasping voice, snatched the shoes by the laces, bellowing as he hauled on them, "Scree! Git the bag! I'll throw the shoes!"

Scree nodded with an insane smirk and darted into the shadows, seeming to melt into the darkness as a battle raged on the other side of the alley.

Two urchins were tugging at my bag, one grunting, "Leggo, Scrunty! Imma takin' this bag!" as the other sneered, "No way, Shrugly! Cloth's good eatin." They had latched on to both ends of the bag and were wrenching at it in opposite directions, straining the coarse fabric.

Meanwhile, Scree, who had reappeared behind the two still bearing his smug expression, lurked like a raven about to feast, ready to scavenge the remnants of the battle.

After I managed to rearrange my wits, I bared my teeth savagely and growled, hoping that I looked threatening enough. At once, all turmoil ceased; the boys wheeled and scrambled from the alley. Unfortunately, they took my bag and shoes with them. They disappeared into another network of side streets, cackling gleefully. In another moment, they'd probably be back to quarreling over my things.

Shaking my head, I stepped from the alleyway and onto a narrow road strewn with urban debris, emerging from the cramped crevice feeling no more rested than I had the night before. I winced as the soles of my bare feet settled onto a layer of soot, Styrofoam restaurant packaging and rubble, hoping that at least one person would be accommodating in this disastrous city. I squinted up at the sky. Hideous black streaks stared back down at me through an ochre haze. Even here, at the very edge of the city, the pollution was awful.

I found myself wandering down the same lattice of alleyways as the boys who had stolen my things. I didn't expect to rediscover those particular urchins, and I figured my possessions were lost forever. I avoided the smallest, gloomiest alleys and the ones from which suspicious noises emerged.

My every step seemed to crunch, impale or squelch on something, and before long my feet were as battered as the rest of me. Nobody stepped forth from the narrow passageways to greet or confront me. Occasionally, I could hear the sounds of the homeless and the orphaned shuffling aside as I passed. Some of these destitute souls scrabbled in my wake and prodded through the blanket of crusted filth on the ground as if hoping I'd dropped something, but I sensed no pursuers.

Eventually, with my feet bruised and coated in grime, I happened across a narrow alley which was filled with the odour of aging raw fish, and my mouth automatically watered despite my revulsion. Under normal circumstances, I would have access to better food which I could simply scavenge in the woods. Here, however, I hadn't come across a single edible thing yet, and I was getting really hungry.

Entering the alley I found the source of the odour: a poorly-gutted fish that looked and smelled long past its prime. The fishy morsel been cast carelessly down onto a nondescript plastic folding table. The table was pressed against the wall of a building alongside a gaping dumpster. The dumpster, table and fish were all humming with flies.

Warily, I approached the table, eyeing the fish carcass splayed across it, its eyes staring sightlessly. I made a quick assessment, judging that anyone from Halftree Village would have cleaned that fish more thoroughly and neatly, then roasted it so it was ready eat in a matter of minutes after it had been caught. They wouldn't abandon a perfectly good fish on a rickety table in some alleyway seething with bacteria. However, my hunger overwhelmed my common sense, and I reached for the fish.

A firm, cold voice erupted from behind me, causing me to spin in alarm on my tender feet:

"Hey! That's my fish. None of you useless urchins are getting my fish!"

Even as I whirled, peering through the shifty light, a young, scraggy girl with dirty limbs and a flinty expression stomped purposefully out of the shadows, baring her teeth at me. She clenched a nasty-looking knife in one scarred hand, and her other hand was bunched into a fist. The youth could clearly detect that I had nothing to defend myself with, for she slashed at the air in front of her with her knife threateningly.

"Get out. Stupid wanderer. Find your own alley, unless you want your face to meet my knife."

Horrified by the weapon, I slowly lowered my hands and backed away, trying to look as non-threatening as possible. These city kids were downright feral!

"O---okay," I stammered, keeping my eyes on that grimy blade, wondering how I could be at the mercy of a girl so much younger than me.

Finally, the girl closed her knife and pocketed it, gaze wandering over to the table and its battered fishy occupant.

"Better not have touched my fish," she hissed, stalking towards the table to examine the dead fish suspiciously. As she continued muttering to herself, I eased my back against a brick building and sidled into the gloom, making my way out of the alley so I could vanish into the skein of litter-strewn roads. Though I was still famished, I didn't want to face that girl's wrath.

Despairing, I had no idea how I would solve the world's problems with an empty stomach. I didn't even know where I was going!

Finally, after wandering the maze of alleyways without further incident, I burst out onto a sidewalk lining a major thoroughfare. Glancing up at the sky to gain my bearings, I discovered that it was nearly impossible to determine what the sun's position was through the veil of thick smog. The roadway was practically deserted. Hardly anyone could be seen making their way along the filth-encrusted walkway, and I had noticed no moving vehicles of any sort. There were a few rusted-out hulks that must have once been cars; these seemed to be lived in by someone now, judging by the piles of blankets and other rubbish that filled their interiors.

Four squat, slim figures lurked beneath a splintered, grubby awning affixed to a building nearby. I squinted at them and spotted the familiar strap of my bag dangling from the hand of one of the figures. The youths appeared to be muttering to each other, one in a recognizably shrill, prattling voice that was rather obnoxious. *That sounds like that kid Trashbag!* Recognising these youths as the thieves who had snatched my possessions, I straightened and crept closer to the outcropping, hoping to overhear what they were talking about.

"Why don't we just sell them loots? Huh? Huh? We don't have to bring 'em to the Master!"

Trashbag was whining softly, watery-blue eyes darting, still clutching my dirty shoes almost protectively to his scrawny chest. I attempted to appear casual and nondescript as I eavesdropped, hoping the urchins wouldn't recognise me.

"We could sell 'em t' Master's… err… whuddyacallits, oh yeah that's right employees!" The boy appeared to be growing more excited by the moment.

"Shaddup, Trashbag," a voice I recognized as T.E.E.'s growled. With that commanding demeanour, he seemed to be the leader of the group, though perhaps he was just the oldest.

"The boss is *right inside* this buildin'. We all know the plan-- give 'im the loot, an' then run fer it. Never know when the thugs from Green-Ware or that CEO what'shisname, Moneybags, is gonna show up-- been awfully mean of late, goin' t'all the gangs an' puttin' 'em outta action. Heard the CEO's gonna tryta drive out all our gangs an' replace 'em with cor'prate thugs, Old Moneybags is, rivalling the boss of Green-Ware himself. Part'a his *great plan* t'set up that mine right next'a the river up north an' dump all the junk in there, I hear."

Mine? I started at this news, realising that the urchins had just given me a clue. Whoever that man was, maybe he had something to do with my visions.

"Scree's *still* scoutin' around in the buildin' t'check for danger? Takin' awful long…" Shrugly remarked, frowning. "Hope he didn't get inta trouble…"

"Right here," an arrogant voice drawled behind my right shoulder, causing me to startle and spin-- how had anyone gotten there without my notice? Surely enough, Scree skulked behind my back, a pair of chipped knives in his hands. To my horror, he was grinning insanely and waggling his knives.

"Coupla nasties in there. Nuthin' serious. Still, prob'ly not a good idea to go in at this point," the boy smirked to the others, attention still focused on me. "Looks like girlie here wants to go in, though…"

Ignoring the urchin's comment and the shouts of, "Hey! How'd ya get there!" from the others, I whirled and ran for the second time that day, grimacing at the pain in my poor tender feet. I headed down one of the alleyways at random, and I didn't slow down until I had thoroughly lost myself in the labyrinth.

Plodding, almost limping, unsure of where to turn for help, I rounded yet another corner and was greeted by a massive mound of discarded, soiled diapers. Streaked with stains, the refuse reeked of excrement and was swarming with insects. A young man sat astride the mound of diapers picking through the wads of cloth, a bag slung over one shoulder. He looked up at me, startled, then a familiar sheepish grin split his face.

"Ferret?" I called out in disbelief, unable to process the thought of finding one of the erstwhile sasquatch hunters here in the city. Though it had been two years since the sasquatch hunters had sought their fortune in the Halftree Village area, this young man hadn't changed much. His narrow face, with its sharp nose and weak jaw, was unmistakable, as was his twitchy habit.

His face flinched in recognition, eyes darting, as I weaved my way over to him through the filth. "Uh... hi." Ferret stammered, not making eye contact and half-sidling away. "Why aren't you back at the village?"

I was so relieved to find a familiar face, I found myself sharing my story. Cautiously at first, then with more enthusiasm as I realized he was really listening, I sketched out the details of my plight. Soon he had heard everything from my haunted dreams to the disastrous events of that morning.

As I spoke, Ferret's mouth crooked into a troubled line.

"Um… yeah. That Old Moneybags those people talked about… he's probably Charles Charleston, CEO of Charles Charleston Inc. There are billboards about his 'project' all over the city. Maybe you haven't seen those yet. He's pretty stuck-up, thinks the homeless and gangs are annoying without realising that the city is kinda sorta made up of homeless and gangs… "

"What project? What billboards?" I asked, frowning.

The young man scratched his scalp and twitched a little, looking indecisive. Finally, he seemed to make up his mind. With a sigh, he rose and beckoned for me to follow him down the street.

10. Charleston Inc.

"How long do you think we have before their 'project' begins? And what is it anyways? If it has to do with the village, then we'll need to do something about it soon," *Besides,* I thought, *we have other things to hide. Things we didn't want anyone catching wind of. Things like Estella's beloved Saska...* Nonetheless, I wasn't naive enough to trust Ferret with that information, not with his history. Some things are best kept secret.

Ferret shuffled a little, glancing around apprehensively as if he was afraid someone would hear him, then finally hissed under his breath, "I guess you'll hafta see the billboards." He darted off down the alley, leaving the steaming pile of diapers behind. I followed him around a corner, but when I got there, no-one was in sight, not even Ferret. I I blinked in confusion before spotting him lurking further down the alley, barely visible in the gloom.

"Ferret!" I called. The scrawny figure started, then scurried back towards me, expression sheepish.

"Why did you… Never mind," I said in disgust as the ex-sasquatch hunter ducked his head in embarrassment. He'd obviously been hoping to lose me. "Show me this billboard you mentioned."

Ferret nodded, then spun and hurried back down the alley. He clearly wanted to get this over with as quickly as possible. I followed in his wake, my tender, bare feet disturbing piles of rubbish.

Before long, we had made our way back to the main street. Ferret halted before a large press-board slab supported by a wooden frame and glanced back at me expectantly. The wooden construct didn't look like much from this side, but I rounded it to see that its face was painted with rows of brightly coloured bulldozers that resembled children's toys. The equipment was arrayed before a scenic background of obviously fake trees. At the top of the billboard, in curly, sparkling golden letters, were the words *Charles Charleston Gold Quarries- The Best New Investment Opportunity Coming To You Soon!* Next to this was a caption above a map that stated, in darker amber lettering, *The Site of the Project!* I squinted at the tiny map, unsure of what to suspect.

Something about the map looked familiar to me. It showed a wooded valley surrounded by mountains, the river running through it, and a small waterfall in the foreground...

My village!

I stumbled back in alarm, eyes wide, and turned on Ferret. He was in the act of slinking away, but froze as soon as he realised that I had noticed him, and gave me a woeful look that seemed to say, *It's not my fault…*

He beckoned to me again, looking resigned. I followed him through the warren of alleys until he ducked under a low doorway. Apprehensively, I looked up and down the alley before following him inside the rickety shack.

"I guess I can try and explain. Umm… There's things and stuff I kinda found about the CEO," Ferret muttered to me. Twitching nervously, he was perched on a splintering wicker chair. I sat in a similar chair, my feet still unclad and scraping against the stained floor.

I nodded distractedly at his vague explanation, my gaze unfocused. *Alright… so I have to pry this out of him. I'm fine with that.*

"I take it Charleston wants to mine for gold around my village?" I snapped at him. He nodded, waving his hand dismissively.

"Strip mining, that's the least of it. He'll use the mine site as a toxic waste dump too." Ferret seemed to know an awful lot about this for an outsider.

"How do you know all this?" I demanded.

"It's common knowledge. Nobody wants chemicals gettin' dumped near the city. People are happy if it all just disappears, even if it is gettin' dumped upstream." The young man's voice was heating up. It seemed we'd hit on a topic that he actually cared about!

I prodded, hoping to get more of a rise out of him. "So how can you just sit here and do nothing about it? There has to be a way to stop this!"

"Yeah," he said, "that's why I'm workin' for the eco-trolls now. We can't shut'em down but at least it's somethin'."

"Eco-trolls?"

"The eco-trolls, um, we do pranks n stuff, make the CEO's lives miserable if we can. Toilet paper their cars, stuff like that. We're targetin' Green-Ware right now."

"So, is Charleston Inc. the leading company in the city, or not? I heard some boys mention Green-Ware earlier today. Is Green-Ware part of this too? I need to know exactly who my enemies are."

Ferret winced. "Green-Ware practically controls the city," he finally managed, fidgeting. "Charleston is sorta new, which is why the eco-trolls never really looked at it before now. Anyways, I'm pretty sure that Charleston will be the one running this city soon."

I groaned wearily as I considered the absurd notion of trying to rally enough citizens to overthrow two powerful corporate antagonists. How else could I shut down the plan to mine Halftree Village?

"I gotta get going," Ferret said, shuffling.

"That's all you can tell me?" I barked at him, frustrated.

95

"Well…" His eyes were on his shuffling feet. "I guess there's one thing. I don't think it will help though." As I continued scowling at him, he finally relented, looking over at me. "Remember Kurt? From the sasquatch hunting crew, the bossy one?" With my answering, angry nod of recognition, he continued. "I… think he's Charleston's son. He found some gold up there somewhere maybe and brought news of it back to the old coot… yeah. Things went up pretty fast."

"You think I can track down Kurt?" I figured it wouldn't hurt to find the man and see if he had any influence.

"Umm, I think he's workin' at the sasquatch exhibit. Just follow the main street downtown, you'll see the signs." Ferret jumped to his feet and headed for the door. "See ya round," he said, hastily.

"Thanks, I guess I'll go try and save the village on my own now," I growled insincerely, then noticed simultaneously both my bare feet and Ferret's new sturdy shoes. "But the least you could do is give me your shoes."

Without hesitation, the ex-sasquatch hunter reached down and wrenched off his shoes, then flung them towards me and hurried off without a backwards glance. "The socks too!" I bellowed after him just as he dashed through the doorway. He peeled them off, and the two linty, limp socks slapped onto the floor. One whiff of them was enough for me; I decided to go without. I wedged the shoes on, wincing at how they chafed my battered feet, and stalked away.

* * *

I retraced my steps to the billboard, then followed the main street towards the heart of the city. Though the street was deserted at first, as I got closer to downtown, merchants with carts and even the occasional traditional shop appeared along the roadway. There were a few locals out buying goods, but they were outnumbered by the scroungers who dug through trash heaps or just sat around looking at the merchant carts hopefully.

The city centre was made up of a cluster of multi-story buildings, and was in much better repair than the area I had just passed through. There were just as many scroungers here, but there were more well-off looking people, all moving quickly as if they were urgently needed elsewhere. I caught a few furtive glances my way, but nobody met my eye.

I spotted a large sign propped beside a flight of stone steps:

This week only! Sasquatch exhibit. Photos! Taxidermy!

Oh dear. Taxidermy? Had they actually killed and stuffed a sasquatch?

This was bad.

I forgot all about the gold mine for a moment, and barged up the steps angrily towards a set of heavy, carved wooden doors.

Museum of Man and Nature, read the proud lettering atop the door-frame.

97

Pushing on the door, I entered a huge chamber with high ceilings. This was the largest building I had ever been inside, and I paused momentarily, awed. The chamber was filled with golden light, cast by countless globe-shaped glass lanterns which were mounted in clusters around the room. The floor was made of slabs of rough grey stone, and the walls were panelled with dark oiled wood. The air smelled like old books.

The room was ringed with mounted photos, all of which appeared to be horribly blurry, and there were a few glass cases which held items on display. One tall glass case stood at the far end of the room; it held a huge bipedal creature. Beside it stood a young man in an official-looking blue suit and hat, both of which were adorned with gold buttons and braids. I stalked up to him, huffing, ready to vent my anger about the hapless creature in the glass case.

Then I got a better look at the creature.

It was quite funny, really.

In spite of the plaque before the creature which read *"Genuine sasquatch! First ever captured"*, the figure looked nothing like Saska. It was obviously made out of some waxy substance, shaped to resemble a large gorilla, and bedecked with mangy tufts of fur that might have been taken from a sickly goat. It was impossible to tell whether it was supposed to be male or female, as the genital area was covered by a particularly large snarl of fur, and the chest was poorly proportioned. The lips were peeled back to show a set of large, yellowed teeth that betrayed the skull as that of a bear.

Despite myself, I snorted with amusement.

Beside me, the man in the blue suit cleared his throat. "Do you have a ticket?" I turned and met his cold, pale eyes; I realised I knew this man. It was Kurt, the erstwhile sasquatch hunter.

Seeing his familiar, unfriendly face recalled me to my mission. *The gold mine!*

"Kurt!" I demanded. He looked taken aback, as he clearly hadn't recognised me. "What's this about a gold mine at my village?"

At that, at least he had the decency to look guilty.

"Anyone can stake a claim," he replied, cagily. "I got there first, is all. My pa is mining the claim."

"What do you mean, you got there first? There are people living there!" I was starting to heat up, and he backed away a step. "And what do you mean, he is mining the claim? *Already?* You have to stop him!"

Kurt shook his head apologetically. "Too late now. The equipment is on its way. The mine will be active by next week."

I raised a fist at him and shook it, furious, though I knew it was pointless trying to convince him of anything. I was too late!

I felt a hand on my shoulder and turned to find another blue-suited man behind me, much larger and burlier than Kurt. He had a no-nonsense look about him.

"Can I see your ticket, miss?"

I blinked at him, innocently, then I spun past him and bolted for the door.

"Hey!" I heard the guard bellowing behind me. He chased me to the door; I didn't turn to look, but the scuff of his shoes sounded awfully close. I pushed the door open wide and let it slam behind me.

Then I ran.

I didn't stop running until I was back on the edge of town, with its abandoned vehicles, dust devils and oil spills. There, lying on some cracked asphalt, were the tattered remains of my bag. Sadly, I collected it and started walking in the direction of the village. Someone had tossed out some crusts of bread and withered slices of ham; I gathered them and stuffed them into the bag just in case I couldn't find anything better to eat along the way.

I was done with this city. I had found answers to my questions here, but no solutions. If there was a way to save the village, it would have to be found in the village itself. If only I could get there before the miners arrived!

11. Cannibal piggies!

I followed the course of the river back upstream, passing through farmland into the dry, sandy region where the hulks of abandoned homesteads loomed ominously. The shrivelled oak saplings, sandy hills and mottled streaks that marked the feral pigs rushing past me merged into a blur. I ended the day's trek by simply collapsing against a dun sand dune, exhausted and hungry.

As the sky darkened, the moon rose, majestic and silver on the horizon, bathing the dusty ground's curves in its glow. My stomach growled hopefully; I hadn't eaten properly in two days. I examined the bread crusts and sliced ham which I'd gathered at the city's outskirts, but found them to be mouldy. I tossed them over the dune in disgust.

I tucked the ragged cloth scrap that remained of my bag under my head and settled down to sleep. When I awoke, the dusky morning light stung my eyes. I wondered if I'd picked up an infection or somehow damaged my vision in the city. Looking around, I saw that the mouldy food that I'd discarded was gone. In its place were several hoof prints and a few pig droppings, smooth olive ovals scattered across the sand. I felt slightly sick. *Cannibal pigs, indeed.*

Over the course of the next day, all signs of the pigs vanished entirely. The landscape became more lush, the soil richer, and the vegetation evolved from stunted oaks to looming pines.

I would reach Hillbilly Falls soon. It would probably be wise to avoid Maggie's hut and find another route around the area. However, there was a chance that I could find something to eat at Maggie's place. Finally, I decided that I would cut straight past her house, in hopes of scavenging a few potatoes and maybe an egg, but I would avoid any contact with her if possible.

As night fell, the area grew increasingly familiar. The groves of evergreen trees each seemed memorable in its own gnarled way, raising broken branches like dusty wings. Crossbills hopped from twig to twig, their crooked overlapping beaks coaxing a smile onto my face.

Finally, I reached the familiar threshold of Maggie's clearing; I could see her house off to the side, the door propped open, ancient hams dangling from the rafters by curly red ribbons. The chickens clucked and squawked noisily in their coop, while the pig pen looked dirtier and more occupied than before. The gate to the pen hung ajar and was spattered with mud. I was startled when a tusked face grinned out at me from the pen's entrance.

It was a boar, enormously fat, his piggy lips pulled into a smirk. He trotted smugly out from the pen, vanishing into the underbrush with a rustle of leaves, his greasy pelt hanging loose from his skin. As I stared after him, a shrieking Maggie burst from the house, waving her broom, eyes wild with rage.

"Cannibal piggies!" she screamed at the boar's fleeing backside, then her rolling eyes focused on me. "Girl. Where you been? C'mere right now! There's work to be done!"

I darted back into the forest as Maggie shrieked, "Girlie! Git back here!"

As I rushed off into the trees, I nearly collided with Ethan, drawing back in alarm just in time. He smiled rather ruefully at me, his arms filled with chopped kindling.

"Elena!" Dropping his burden, he embraced me in his broad muscular arms, then withdrew, studying me. "You look tired. Are you okay?"

I ignored his question, instead asking, "What are you doing here?"

He looked abashed. "I wanted to rescue you… but Maggie got to me first. She set me onto doing chores right away, and made me capture a pig for her to put in her pen. I'm scared to leave-- she's insane! If I don't bring this firewood back she'll hit me in the head with her evil broom again! I-- "

"Don't be absurd," I groaned, exasperated. "Come on." I grabbed his arm and hauled him stumbling after me, forcing him through the bushes, widely skirting Maggie's clearing. He protested loudly, but I silenced him by saying, "You found me, didn't you?" He reluctantly followed me, rubbing his arm and grumbling.

Before long, we reached Hillbilly Falls. The waterfall seemed imposing as it roared down the slope. The cliff-like riverbank looked impossibly steep, so climbing it was out of the question. "We'll have to find some alternate way up," I said to Ethan, suddenly feeling dizzy and fatigued. "But right now, I need to get some sleep."

"Maggie-- " Ethan began, but I interrupted him.

"Bad idea. We'll sleep somewhere else, *anywhere* else. If we go back there then we're doing chores for the rest of our lives, and not particularly pleasant ones."

"Fine," the man agreed bitterly, his tone making a pang of sorrow shoot through me. I could feel the distance between us, as indestructible as a wall. I never knew why we did drift apart. Then I shook the thought off, and gestured for him to follow me as I looked for a sheltered spot where we could rest for the night.

I awoke beside Ethan to the joyful chorus of songbirds. I rolled upright in the small nook where we had rested for the night, glanced down at Ethan to see that he was still asleep and snoring softly, then I lifted my tattered bag. It was woefully empty.

I was able to pick a few raspberries nearby, over-ripe and withered, but tasty nonetheless. I ate my share as Ethan slowly and groggily awoke. As he rose, stooping beneath the overhanging bushes, I offered the remaining berries to him; wordlessly, he took them.

Once our meagre breakfast had been finished, we left the hollow, looking up at the churning river as it tumbled down towards us. The early sunlight glimmered off the water's surface, dancing crimson like tongues of fire.

"I'm still hungry," Ethan finally complained, breaking the silence. "We should go and eat at Maggie's house-- "

"Nope," I said automatically, even as the seed of an idea germinated in my mind. "But we need food… Wait. You just inspired me. Let's sneak over to Maggie's house, raid her garden and run before she wakes up." As soon as the words left my mouth, I heard their brash recklessness and raised my hand to my mouth, but Ethan's eyes lit up at the prospect of raiding the old woman's hut. Besides, there was really no other option unless we were to rely on berries for our survival.

We started padding silently down the hill. Wordlessly, I signed to Ethan to approach from the left; I kept to the right, edging through the trees and trying not to disturb the bushes so that my approach would be soundless. The scarlet sunrise confused my vision; random chaotic bands of shadow dappled the soil through the dull jade needles of the pines. From my position, I knew, I was angling down towards the chicken coop, while Ethan moved towards the empty pig pen and the garden tucked snugly behind it. My task would be the most challenging-- to collect some eggs without causing the chickens to sound an alarm-- but after that, I could continue on to help Ethan dig up potatoes.

The back of Maggie's house reared into sight; for once, it looked unoccupied. No smoke streamed from the chimney, so it seemed likely that she was still in bed. As I had hoped, the chickens were also asleep, safely nestled in the straw with their heads tucked under their wings.

I snuck towards the gate and rattled the latch lightly; it was unlocked. Warily pushing it open with a soft creak, I crept into the coop, careful not to rouse any of the chickens.

Now came the most difficult part-- stealing the eggs. I managed to slide a few of the slick, pale ovals out from beneath the chickens with only a few disgruntled clucks, holding my breath as I did so, then pushed them into my bag delicately. Then I inched out of the coop, easing the gate shut behind me. The latch slid closed with a soft click.

Even as I began to skulk across the clearing towards Maggie's hidden garden, an uproar of clacking and squawking exploded from the chickens. The outraged birds pecked and clawed ferociously at the mesh, enraged that I would dare steal their eggs.

A rattle came from the door of the cabin, and a familiar voice wheezed, "Who be touchin' mah chickens? They dem cannibal piggies?"

As the door creaked open: "Settle down, ya darn chickens! Can't anyone git any rest round here?"

I ran from the coop back towards the river, clutching my bag to my chest protectively.

As I caught my breath, panting, I listened for Ethan's return. At first there was no sign of him, and I started to worry. What if Maggie had caught him? I was torn between worry and anger-- afraid that he was in trouble, and annoyed that he would worry me so.

I sighed with relief when he finally emerged from the dark-spattered forest. A roughly woven potato sack was slung over his shoulder, and the leafy tops of potato plants poked through its mouth. His hands were dirty, and his expression was resigned and exhausted. I couldn't decide whether to hug him or growl at him for worrying me, so I did neither. Instead, I reached out to take the potatoes.

"Hardly any of the good ones left," he explained, handing me the bag. "The ones near the surface were all rotted through. I had to dig deep to find these."

"Let's go look for a way up," I said, unsure of how to respond. Ethan nodded agreement, content to let me take the lead. I put the potatoes in my bag and carefully nestled the eggs on top of them, abandoning the bulky potato sack, then we began striding along the riverbank's base. I felt a bit weak and queasy, but I assumed it was just due to my hunger and fatigue. We'd be able to eat something once we got further away from Maggie's homestead.

The cliff-face where the river rushed down the slope was far too sheer for us to climb, so we entered the deeper forest, hoping the cliff would grow shallower and rockier with more hand and footholds.

The towering trees were gloomy and ominous, sending muted light sifting down like dust between their branches. The moss underfoot was damp, dark green with the surrounding wetness, and the black soil seemed rich and clean. The haunting hoots of an owl resounded through the trees, making me feel as if this place was sacred to nature and we were trespassing. Ethan must have felt the same way, for we both stepped gently, careful not to disturb the delicate forest floor.

Finally, the cliff and the ground seemed to join together, the huge sharp stones engulfed by the soft, warm earth. The precipice was like a bony spine, a ridge spreading across the land, dotted by immense tall trees. I paused to wait for Ethan to catch up. As he emerged from the deep shadows, we made our way across the precipice and headed back towards the river. The forest was drier across the top of the ridge, less mysterious, returning to twisted stubby pines and hulking knotted spruces. As we neared the river, we paused to look down at Maggie's squat shack so far below, ringed by overgrown trees.

Ethan stood beside me, overlooking the forest. We watched as a chill rain came softly drumming down from the sky. The sun dawned hazily through the thin veil of storm clouds, bathing the shack below, and its occupant, in droplets. Then, as a gentle cool breeze caressed us, we turned and left Hillbilly Falls.

12. Bird fever

The day-long trip from the village to Hillbilly Falls turned out to be a three-day trip going home. Unable to use a raft to travel upstream, Ethan and I had to forge a trail, following the river. While animal trails eased our passage in some areas, we had to cross numerous streams and cut through tangled thickets of willow and brambles.

It was already far after dusk on the third day by the time Ethan and I reached the village, drenched, scratched, and chilled to the bone. The light sprinkling of rain had heralded a fully-fledged storm, complete with raging winds, roiling black clouds and flashes of lightning. The rumble of thunder was constant, and water came pouring down in bucketfuls.

To add to our misery, no ground was dry enough to build a fire on, which meant not only were we horribly chilled but also ravenous, for all the food we had stolen from Maggie's house required cooking-- unless we wanted to slurp uncooked eggs and gnaw on raw potatoes. We had to make do with eating berries, and we took chances with the mushrooms we came across. I regretted not gathering ham from Maggie's rafters, though I'd had enough ham for a lifetime.

Once we had reached the village, the storm had finally ended, leaving us trembling and stumbling. I leaned on Ethan for support, but the man himself was unsteady on his feet, and we both nearly fell as we reached the path between the houses.

The village was still and silent, which made sense for few people wandered aimlessly around at night. "Estella!" I called out, feeling guilty at disturbing my friend at so late an hour. As I'd hoped, Estella peered out from her house, hugging a squirming Emma and a sleepy Erin to her chest. She took one look at me and Ethan, struggling to hold each other upright, then responded, "I'll get help!" and rushed back into the house. I was too exhausted to protest that I didn't want to awaken anyone else.

Estella returned, without the girls, but with a blanket bundled in her arms. As my friend hastened towards me and I staggered free of Ethan only to collapse into Estella's arms, I noticed that the blanket was dark blue and silver, with the glints of silver bright against the murky backdrop. The blue reminded me of the river, with threads of green and paler blues woven into it.

111

I recognized the blanket as one that Nana had made some years back, yet I couldn't put my finger on why it carried new significance for me now.

The blanket was wrapped around me, but I continued staring feverishly at it, imagining sinking into those depths and never returning to the surface. Estella led me into a cabin where the wood stove blazed, yet I could not stop shivering. I plunged into a deeper darkness, and knew nothing more.

I awoke gasping to Nana's scowling, disapproving face. My limbs trembled, my forehead burning with a strange blistering heat. "Fever," Nana harrumphed, waggling a finger. "You should have taken shelter as soon as the storm arrived." She rose, calling to someone I couldn't see, "She's awake."

I tried to sit up, but my muscles went numb and my skin prickled with stinging cold, darkness flooding my vision. I flopped back onto the blanket, defeated, and closed my eyes. Then I remembered why I had returned to the village-- I needed to warn the elders about the fast-approaching mining crew.

We had to stop them! What other option was there? Would we have to evacuate, abandoning our homes? I looked up again to see that Nana was ambling away, grumbling something to herself. "Wait!" I called. She turned and glanced back at me, eyebrow raised.

My entire story of the journey to the city, my learning of Charleston's plan and my voyage home poured from my mouth in a slurred rush. Then, before I could see Nana's reaction to my tale or answer her inevitable questions, I felt the fever overtake me again and sagged back into the blanket, unconscious before my head hit the pillow.

* * *

Nana perched on a log at the edge of the fire pit and watched as Old Jack and Simon shuffled over, hands red and raw from working at the fish camp. Old Jack was scowling, scratching at his long wiry beard as he sat, Simon plunking himself down opposite him and meeting no-one's eyes. Their shifts at the fish camp had been interrupted, and they were both in a foul mood, especially Jack, who'd accidentally cut open his hand when gutting a fish. He held a rag to the wound, his face twisting as he staunched the bleeding.

Myra was already there, and now she spoke in a quavering voice, hunching forwards. "Which of you first wishes to speak?"

Before Nana could say a thing, Old Jack stood up, still scowling. "I will, an' I'm sayin' now that it's a waste a time. There ain't no city folk out ta get us. There can't be. That girl, she was lyin', or delusional, or sumpin' anyways. She wuz fevered. Fever dreams do strange things ta people, put strange thoughts in their heads, things that they wouldn't usually think." He sat back down.

Nana said, "I spoke with Ethan. He said that when he found Elena, she looked tired, not just physically, but spiritually, and she seemed driven to tell us what she had learned."

113

Simon, still looking down at his hands, grumbled wearily. "C'mon, Nana. He's a young man obsessed with a young woman. He'd say she looked tired and driven if she'd just woken up from a good long sleep all comfy and cozy in her bed."

"No," Nana countered, "He'd say she looked beautiful after she finished cleaning the cobwebs out from under the porch, Simon. I remember these things. If he said that she was tired and driven then she was, almost to the point of breaking." She waved a hand. "But that's all beside the point."

"Right," Old Jack said, "we need to prove her wrong-- "

"We don't need to prove anything," Nana retorted. She glared around at the circle of elders: Jack's belligerent stare, Myra's sceptical regard, Simon's ancient eyes that avoided meeting hers. "Remember old Jessie? How he was always prepared for everything? That's the example we need to follow. We need to set a watch on every route into the village. If the miners arrive and they can't be dissuaded, which I'm betting they can't, then we need to call an evacuation."

Myra asked, "All in agreement?"

Jack scowled, but nodded. So did Simon.

Myra raised one feeble hand. "Council dismissed."

* * *

Sheldon Morley huffed as he climbed the low ridge that overlooked the helicopter landing site, his skinny, bowed legs straining at the effort. He had worked as a recruiter for several other job sites and a gang or two before, but this was his first wilderness job. He had signed on with Charleston's mining management team with some trepidation, as he liked his comforts, but the excitement of treading unknown soils convinced him to take the leap.

From the top of the ridge, he could see across the whole valley. The river wound through the forest like a silver ribbon. There, way off in the distance, was a smudge in the air that marked the location of the city. Eyeing that smudge, he felt a sudden swell of homesickness. He wondered how his pet ferrets were doing without him. He hoped they were feeding well on the mice that plagued his housing compound. He shuddered at the thought of those disease-carrying vermin, scurrying about, soiling his counters and floors with their filthy little feet.

If this job paid well enough in bonuses and dividends, he would look into moving to a better housing unit. But then he would have to buy more food for his ferrets. Everything was a trade-off.

Tugging at his wispy hair, he scanned the valley, trying to find the village where they would be making their base camp. He wasn't sure what it would look like. Rustic, for sure. His imagination painted a picture of a squalid camp inhabited by near-feral humans. It amazed him that anyone would actually choose to live out here, amongst the bugs and the bears.

115

As a recruiter, would he find anyone healthy and strong enough to work in the mine? Or would the villagers all be malnourished, stunted and illiterate? He hoped there would be at least a few able bodies, since his pay rate was contingent upon the productivity of the recruits.

Even if the recruitment might be a flop, he had another reason for taking this job. There was another hope for payout, faint as a glimmer, but if it panned out, he would be very wealthy. Just days ago, he had received a mysterious summons from a professor at the university. Curious, he had responded to the anonymous missive, meeting the dark-cloaked professor in a nondescript coffee shop in the student district.

The professor had handed him a bundle of smudged photographs. He told him what to look for. Signs of scat, tufts of fur, the sounds of bellowing, huffing, or strange drumming noises from the deep woods.

Sheldon had been alarmed by the thought of seeing and hearing such things, but he licked his lips and accepted the contract, thinking only of a better future for himself and his beloved pets. Stowed away in his luggage were three crucial pieces of equipment: a camera, a tranquilizer dart gun, and a call beacon. The nameless professor had handed them to him, tied in a slick bundle, and he had made one thing very clear. A photograph of a sasquatch would pay Sheldon's way out of the slums. A captured sasquatch would buy his way into a gated community.

If this gambit worked out, he would be very, very wealthy indeed.

116

"Sheldon!" One of the tough-looking mine guards was calling him down off the ridge.

Throat bobbing, Sheldon piped a reply. "Coming!" He tried to pitch his voice lower when talking to those thugs, but it still sounded reedy to his own ears. He wished he had a more intimidating voice. The voice says a lot about the man, his father had always said. His father was the type of person whose presence filled a whole room. He never had to worry about his voice squeaking or cracking.

Sheldon ducked his head and wove his way back down the hill. Though he wished his voice would boom like his father's had, he was proud to be one of the fore-runners, the group that would make first contact and prepare for the arrival of the miners. It was just him and the four guards for now; the rest of the mining crew would be arriving next week. He knew he was good at his job; he was chosen for this role over other, more experienced recruiters. He felt competent and necessary.

And now, it was time to set up a rudimentary camp for the night. He wasn't looking forward to a night of sleeping on the hard ground, so close to the crawling insects and other vermin.

Tomorrow, they would mark a route to the village with flagging tape, in preparation for the tree-cutters and road-builders who would arrive with the next influx of Charleston's employees.

Soon, this infernal, bug-infested bush would be tamed.

117

13. Intruders

The village youth had infiltrated the countryside, ringing the village with sentinels, hoping to catch sight of the approaching miners to give the villagers some advance warning. Runt had proposed this, as a precaution, and he was quietly proud that the elders had accepted his proposal. As a newcomer to the village, city-born, he valued their trust in him all the more. He had tried so hard to fit in, then that fiasco with the sasquatch in Estella's cabin had really set him back. He still felt foolish, and his cheeks felt hot as he recalled the scene.

Runt had chosen to keep an eye on the spot where his old sasquatch hunting crew had arrived: a flat ridge overlooking the river, where a helicopter could conveniently land. He had chosen well, He was the first to spot the fore-runners as they struggled to pitch their tents below the ridge, hands flapping to dispel the biting insects which swarmed them hungrily. The stocky young man ran back to the village, puffing, to alert everyone to the intruders.

"City people! They are setting up camp, up on the river ridge!" His cry alerted the villagers who scurried to gather around the central hearth pit. A decision would have to be made, quickly. Would they try to repel the intruders? Or would they abandon their homes, evacuating the village to preserve their chosen way of life?

Nana nodded at Runt in acknowledgement, then signed to him through the throng of milling villagers. They had planned this part earlier. He was to go back to the intruders, see what he could learn about their intentions, and infiltrate them if he could.

He retraced his steps, quietly approaching the river ridge. The evening was rapidly fading into darkness, and the moon, a narrow waning crescent, had not yet risen. Keeping to the shadows, he was able to get quite close to the intruders, their roaring campfire blinding them to everything around them.

There were five of them in total. Three huge men and a tough looking woman sat on a fallen log on one side of the fire. They were all of the type known as 'enforcers' in the city; enforcers were hired on for every job that required guarding or bullying. They wore camouflage jackets and rugged pants, and their belts were adorned with the tools of the trade: flashlights, mysterious buckled pouches, and billy clubs. Runt wondered why this job required so much muscle. Apparently, Charleston was expecting some trouble.

The fifth and final member of the group was a gangly little fellow with a shock of wispy white hair. He sat apart from the others, and he looked terribly uncomfortable. Smoke from the fire was drifting right into his face. The little man blinked and coughed, squinting over at the others.

"Git yerself outta the smoke, Sheldon," remarked the woman. She patted the log beside her, flashing a predatory smile. "Or would you prefer a nice, soft bed in the village? Don't worry, we'll have you one of those by tomorrow."

Sheldon cleared his throat then piped, "Less bugs over here. Anyway, I've got to check on something." He scurried off into one of the tents, which had been erected haphazardly around the clearing.

Runt circled around behind the tent. He could hear Sheldon muttering to himself: *"Thugs, idiots, know nothings, she's gonna eat me alive.….. gold anyway, when are the machines gonna arrive, hope it's in time…. get out this equipment, hope those idiots didn't break anything… check the bushes, sasquatch country, Ha!"*

Sasquatch country? Oh no! Runt watched in horror as the little man slunk out of his tent, hunched over, armed with a flashlight and a camera. Worse still, Sheldon had a tranquilizer gun strung over one shoulder! Runt hoped the thing would go off and hit Sheldon accidentally.

Cautiously, Runt backed away from the campsite, avoiding the bushes where Sheldon had begun poking about with his flashlight. Sheldon swatted at unseen insects, cursing. The camera swung about on its neck strap colliding with the tranquilizer gun. He cursed again.

"What the heck are you up to over there, little Sheldon? Think you're gonna recruit some of the wildlife?" growled one of the enforcers. The others laughed roughly as Sheldon turned back towards them, looking sheepish.

The sound of their cruel laughter haunted Runt as he hurried back towards the village to sound the alarm.

FOUR enforcers and a recruiter? Runt was appalled; those enforcers were like militia. They did not mean to negotiate their way into the village. And the recruiter was looking for signs of a sasquatch. This was really, really bad!

* * *

The council did not take Runt's news lightly. They put the evacuation plan into motion; the villagers would hold on as long as they could, playing along with the recruiter, but they would evacuate with the arrival of the first of the machinery. They just couldn't sit back and watch their way of life destroyed.

The sun was high in the sky the next day when the fore-runners entered the village, looking battered, tired and miserable. Apparently it had been a rough night; not one of them was used to sleeping outdoors, and biting insects had made short work of them. They must have bush-whacked the whole way to the village, judging by the scratches on their faces and arms. There were easier ways to get through the woods, making use of animal trails and exposed ridges, but not knowing any better, they took a more difficult route, likely following the line of a compass.

The villagers showed no surprise at the arrival of the five intruders, instead offering a round of introductions and a noontime meal by the central fire pit. The four enforcers looked sullen, and somewhat taken aback that their brawn wasn't immediately called for. The recruiter, Sheldon, just looked relieved to sit down and have a bite to eat. He looked the most bedraggled of them all; the mosquitoes must have found him especially tasty. Either that, or he had spent a good part of the night out of his tent, where the insects happily devoured him.

Ethan sat down next to the recruiter, clopping him on the shoulder with one large, meaty hand. Sheldon was nearly bowled over, but he cleared his throat and offered the young man a sheepish smile.

"You look like a nice strong lad. Looking for work?"

"Not at the moment," Ethan replied. "We'll see." The villagers had agreed to gently refuse all offers of working for the mine, while maintaining the impression that they weren't hostile to the idea. They didn't want the enforcers to get involved, if at all possible.

Right now, those enforcers didn't look very interested in roughing anyone up. The villagers knew, though, that the situation would change if they were aggravated in any way, or even if they got too bored. Ethan and several other youths had been charged with making sure that didn't happen. They were to chat with the intruders, show them around, and try to get them engaged in the activities that were integral to village life. "Keep'em busy, get those hands doing something. Get'em catching n' gutting fish. Then they won't have time to make no trouble," as Old Jack had put it. The youths had put them up in the communal cabin, billeting the cabins usual residents in the homes of other villagers. Then they set about trying to find hobbies for the newcomers.

As the youths soon learned, the intruders weren't much interested in anything to do with village life. At first, they just wanted to be fed and to have soft beds to sleep in. As the days went on, as their welts healed and they got caught up on sleep, they became harder to distract.

The recruiter Sheldon pretty much kept to himself, apart from repeatedly offering all the young, healthy villagers the opportunity to work in the mine. He seemed preoccupied with exploring the bush around the village, armed with a camera and a strange looking gun. Runt had mentioned that the equipment was likely for sasquatch hunting, but the little recruiter seemed hesitant to venture far from the village. This was probably a good thing, as nobody much relished the thought of having to send out a search party for him.

Runt watched Sheldon's sasquatch hunting efforts and wondered, for a moment, just how much the man would pay him to share what he knew. He quickly dismissed the thought. No amount would be enough for him to betray the villagers in that way. He had come here as an outsider, and they had welcomed him with open arms, accepting him as one of their own. He had never felt such a sense of belonging until he moved here. He had left the cut-throat world of the city behind, and he had no regrets at all.

Though Sheldon had found a way to occupy himself, the four enforcers were another matter. Two of them, identified by the names embroidered on their identical camouflage jackets as Cooper and Jonas, spent most of their spare time fiddling with the small electronic devices which they stored lovingly in their belt pouches. That distraction soon lost its lustre, as the devices ran out of power on the third day of their stay in the village. With horror, the two thugs then discovered that the village was without power. The demise of their electronic devices left the two moping about like lost souls, and the elders feared they would soon start causing trouble.

The other enforcers were called Leaf and Knife. That is, the woman insisted with a growl that everyone call her Knife, though her jacket identified her as Skinner. She was the fiercest of the lot; even Sheldon tried to steer clear of her, and she teased him relentlessly. Ethan had tried to make conversation with her on the first day, but she repelled his friendly gesture with a glare, drawing her belt knife then turning to sharpen it on a whet stone. She scowled about, as if daring anyone else to try and approach her. They left her alone after that.

Leaf was the only enforcer that had picked up anything like a hobby from the villagers. On the second evening by the central fire, he had watched with some interest out of the corner of his eye as Ethan sat whittling a little wooden bear from a piece of dry wood. The next day, he could be seen hacking at sticks with the cruel looking knife he had drawn from his own belt, though it was hard to tell what he was trying to make. "He's making a dull blade, at any rate," Nana quipped to Estella as they headed to Nana's cabin to start the day's weaving. It was part of the "look busy, act normal" ploy which the villagers had undertaken, in hopes of concealing the fact that they were relocating their village, item by item, to a site some 6 hours upstream. The newcomers seemed unaware that large numbers of villagers were gone for most of the day, taking their personal belongings with them, only to return empty-handed by nightfall.

The villagers were making the move in shifts, keeping a skeleton crew around the village to create the illusion that nothing was awry. When the mining equipment arrived, they intended to leave immediately, leaving nobody behind. Meanwhile, temporary shelters were being hastily erected at the new village site. New cabins would have to be built before winter.

On the sixth day, the recruiter looked particularly haggard and sheepish as he stood surrounded by four grumpy-looking enforcers, watching the logging and mining equipment roll in. He had failed to recruit a single villager, and his obsessive hunt for sasquatches had availed him nothing. Here he was, empty-handed, and the rest of the mining crew had arrived.

14. Evacuation

When the mining equipment arrived, along with a flock of workers who darted about busily establishing a camp site at the south end of the village, the day's evacuation crew had just returned. The villagers were ready to move to their new site.

The elders were confident that the plan would preserve the village way of life and keep the villagers out of harm's way, though they lamented their powerlessness to save the village site itself. After three generations, they were emotionally attached to the familiar landscape, and their comfortable cabins would have to be left behind, with all their history.

Estella did her part to maintain the charade of village life, but her mind was troubled. What, she pondered, could she do about Saska? He was likely still in the area, and Runt's warning about the sasquatch hunter hiding in the midst of the miners really frightened her. She fretted silently, feeling very alone. Nobody else seemed worried about Saska at all!

Then the night after the mining equipment arrived, in the wee hours before the village would begin its mass evacuation, Estella and Nana worked together to dismantle the loom. They would carry it with them to the new village site in the morning. Nana looked across its wooden frame at Estella slyly and said, "What has the weaving taught you?" Estella shook her head, curious to see where Nana was going with this thought.

Nana continued, "Where's the best place to hide the things that are most precious to us? Hide them in plain sight."

That was it! With a grin, Estella strode purposefully from Nana's cabin to her own cabin's hearth, her features set with determination. It was nearing dawn now; Emma was still sound asleep in the warm bed. The fireplace was cold as Estella knelt down before it. With all the excitement of the night before, she had let the fire go out. She reached over and began to dig at the mortar.

As the loose hearthstone was pulled away, she sighed in relief to see that the glossy black stone was still nestled in its little hollow. After a brief examination, she brushed her hair from her face and sat back. The stone was cracked, webbed with tiny fractures that had been invisible to her at first in the dim light. Had the hearth fire damaged it?

Would it still work? Estella hesitated a moment, then cautiously lifted the curious stone and shook the soot from it. The stone gleamed brightly, smooth and black and silver in the light of her lantern. She ran a finger lovingly down its polished surface, then whispered, "Saska. Come." and kissed it. Strangely, this time she could feel a jolt of energy run through her as her lips brushed the stone, and she shuddered, drawing back slightly. Once she had recovered from the initial shock, she dropped the stone into her pouch, patted the hearthstone back into place, and stood.

There was much to prepare for on this grim day. She could only hope that the stone still worked, and that Saska could make his way to the village without being spotted by the intruders.

Because the stone was hidden in her pocket, she did not see the jet-black glow that rose from the cracks in its surface, nor did she hear the tiny splintering sound as something within began to work its way free.

* * *

The call came suddenly in the early hours of morning, an insistent tugging at his attention. Saska plucked a juicy mushroom from the damp patch of earth where he had made his bed the night before. He shoved the tender morsel into his mouth, hardly bothering to chew, and quickly stood, shaking out his shaggy brown pelt.

In a nearby tree, Twitchy woke and chittered inquisitively, and Saska took a moment to toss a mushroom at the little squirrel before turning to run

128

towards the village. Twigs raked his furry arms and became tangled in his hair like the reaching claws of a hungry beast, yet he continued on, driven by the intensity of the call and the knowledge that Estella needed him. She would only have used the stone if her need was desperate.

The sun rose slowly in the east, wreathed in ugly clouds, painting the land in a deathly grey light. He continued forwards, feeling not only as if he were being chased this time, but also as if he were being *pushed*. It was more powerful than the raging current of a river, more frightening than a pack of angry wolves nipping at his heels.

Off to the side, he could see the rust-red form of his squirrel friend lunging from tree to tree, and he smiled to himself, his large teeth a sudden flash of white in his hairy face. The faithful little guy would probably stay at his side until he reached the very edge of the village.

The trees parted, the houses appeared, and, as expected, the squirrel halted, eyed him for a moment, then scurried away. Saska continued on, weaving between the cabins, grateful for the fact that no-one was awake yet.

At the opposite end of the village, he caught a glimpse of bulldozers, steamrollers and other strange machinery parked on a broad swath of dirt where the forest had been unceremoniously cleared away. He felt a cold sense of foreboding trickling down his spine. As he ran, he thought he saw the dull green canvas of tents fluttering in the wind on the square of bare earth. There was a distressing odour of oil and crushed plants in the air.

Finally, Estella's cabin came into view. He slowed to a walk as the call diminished, then vanished entirely. She was waiting for him, he saw, sitting on the porch looking lost and forlorn. She smiled up at him as he approached, but it was a sad smile. As he plopped down heavily next to her, a river of tears started flowing down her cheeks. He leaned lightly against her, his brow furrowed, until the tears stopped and she looked up at him with a deep sigh. She smiled again sadly at his worried expression, then tugged him into the cabin.

"We have to get out of here, and I'm bringing you with me. Put this on." Estella held out a large, hooded shirt and some baggy pants. They were made of a roughly woven fabric, the type that was normally used for sacking. "They are Uncle John's. Hopefully they will fit you?"

Saska, alarmed, pulled back as Estella attempted to draw the hooded shirt over his head. She couldn't reach, and laughing, she stood on the bed and tried again. "Come here, silly! These clothes won't hurt you. We just need to get you past the city people without anyone thinking they can add you to their plunder."

His arms flailed as she tried helplessly to pull the shirt down over his body. Soon she was laughing so hard she collapsed on the bed, barely able to breathe. Blinded by the shirt which was now wrapped awkwardly around his face and neck, Saska continued to flail about, panicking. A sleepy Emma peeped up from under the covers of the bed where she had been sleeping.

Finally, Estella recovered from her furious laughter. She saw that Saska was trying haplessly to tug the shirt down over his body the rest of the way. She exclaimed, "Oh, Saska! It'll take you all day to get it on like that. Here, let me help." She stood, reached over and pulled the shirt down the rest of the way as he struggled to stay as still as possible, then she drew the hood up over his woolly head.

She studied Saska as he moped, his furry face woeful, then said, "Well, it might work if you hunch down a bit. Probably." She held out the pants. "Now for these."

It took an absurd amount of time to squeeze him into the pants. They hung awkwardly from his muscular legs, bunching in strange places, and his woolly pelt stuck out of the top in wiry brown tufts. Estella tried to make the pants look vaguely normal, smoothing out the creases and tucking in the hairs that stuck out across his lower back.

She hopped down from the bed, studying him, then nodded wordlessly. It would have to do. She gathered up a wide-eyed Emma in her arms, and together, Saska slouching and keeping his face down-turned and shadowed, they walked out of the cabin and into daylight.

Before long, they joined a column of villagers, shuffling despondently out from their houses, stirring up clouds of dust as they left their village behind. Saska had never seen so many people in one place, and his eyes darted left and right as he slumped, trying to make himself inconspicuous.

In the sea of sad, weary faces, Estella could see many that she knew. There was Nana, looking stern and determined. There was Elena, who had awakened from her fever sleep only recently and who wore a puzzled expression as she cradled a bedraggled Erin, pointedly *not* leaning on Ethan for support.

After a time, they reached the edge of Halftree Village, where the four enforcers stood. They were clothed in their familiar dull camouflage uniforms, and they had a strictly military look about them today. The recruiter, Sheldon, stood before them, lacking their military look. He was slumped and bow-legged, and he had clearly attempted to make himself look presentable this morning, but a few unruly white wisps of hair surrounded his head like a halo. His bright clothing made a sharp contrast to the uniform green and grey of the enforcers.

"Step right up for recruitment!" The man piped boldly at the villagers as they passed. "We need some strong, healthy backs to join our team! Excellent rewards!"

Estella nodded in approval as Nana and the other elders glared at the man warily, steering the villagers around him. Some of the youngsters looked inquisitive, and Runt was muttering to them and shaking his head. Elena had latched onto Ethan's arm and was possessively pulling him along.

"You there! You look good and sturdy! Step over here please, sir, and we'll get you signed up!" With horror, Estella realised the man was waving towards

Saska, who began to turn his furry face towards him curiously. She hastily snatched his arm and steered him off to the side, away from the recruiter.

"Don't look!" she hissed. "He mustn't see your face!" Emma, riding on Estella's hip, reached over to Saska worriedly, tugging at the bottom of his shirt.

"Papa?"

He looked down at the little girl, grinning broadly at her sweet face. She reached for him and he took her into his arms just as a wild chirping erupted from the nearby trees. A squirrel burst through the greenery, darted over, and ran right up Saska's leg! Emma crowed with delight.

"Twitchy!" scolded Estella. *So much for being unobtrusive,* she thought. By now, everyone was staring at her little party, confusion on the faces of the city people and amusement on those of the villagers.

The wispy-haired recruiter shrieked, his arms flailing. "Vermin! Disease-ridden vermin! Quick, get away!" He scurried off, his bow-legged gait causing him to bob wildly.

Snorting, Estella smiled with relief. At least the recruiter was no longer eyeing Saska. Now they just had those enforcers to worry about. Glancing over, she saw that they were no longer looking her way. Their eyes had traced the wild path of the recruiter, then their expressions fell blank again. One scuffed the dirt with his boot and cleared his throat; another was fiddling with the gear on his belt. Only the woman who called herself Knife looked amused; the others just looked bored.

As Estella steered her little party past the enforcers, one of the men eyed Saska suspiciously. Saska cradled Emma in his arms and awkwardly hunched by the enforcers, Estella tugging him along. Fortunately, the enforcers said nothing, letting them pass. Twitchy continued to cling to Saska's leg, glaring around and scolding everyone in sight. His bushy tail twitched, and his black eyes glittered as he glared at the enforcers. Before long, they were swallowed up in the crowd once more, just another family of refugees evacuating the village, and the enforcers quickly forgot about them.

The villagers streamed into the mountains, weaving between the trees. Saska stared up at the crowd, unable to believe that so many people had been able to fit in so small a village, then glanced back anxiously through the forest to make sure the village was no longer in sight. Twitchy chattered once, then scrambled up onto his head where he perched, surveying the refugees warily.

Suddenly, Estella felt something squirm inside her pocket. She stopped to take a look, feeling a shock run through her. Saska paused, studying her anxiously, and Emma gurgled and curiously stared at her mother. Estella looked down at her pocket, and saw slashes appear in the fabric as if invisible claws had torn it open. The thing trapped within writhed its way free, making a noise that sounded like a triumphant squeal.

134

The creature itself seemed to be nothing but a shadowy outline, and she turned out her pocket to get a better look. The shiny black fragments of the call stone tumbled down to the forest floor. Still, she could not spot the creature that had emerged from the stone. It seemed to be cloaked in shadows. A moment later, lizard-like footprints began to appear in the rich soil, moving swiftly towards the bright silver thread of the river. Then they were gone.

Estella bent down to retrieve the remains of the call stone, then thought better of it and stopped. Some things were best left to nature. She stood up and continued walking, smiling pleasantly at a befuddled Saska and a worried-looking Emma. "It's okay. We didn't need it anymore anyways."

Twitchy chattered his agreement.

* * *

The time passed quickly during the early days after the evacuation. The new village site was a hub of activity as we raced to erect new cabins while the weather was good for building. When I could get away, I spent hours sitting on a high ridge above the new village site overlooking the river, wondering about the mysteries those deep waters held. I also checked frequently on the progress of the mining camp.

The progress of Charles Charleston's workers was swift. They levelled out the ground around the village, razing the undergrowth and knocking down trees. They set up watermills to harness the power of the river, as well as

135

stranger things that would presumably be necessary for their work. All the while, more and more workers arrived with their machinery and supplies, preparing to strip-mine the area for its gold.

On a day just like any other, I stood on high ground overlooking the old village, watching the miners work. Charles Charleston's hirelings milled about like ants in the light of the morning sun, dark blotches against the green and brown of the forest below.

As I despondently watched them go about their day's work, Ethan came up behind me and touched me lightly on the shoulder. I looked up at him, feeling a flash of annoyance. Had he followed me here?

Ethan smiled grimly, then looked back down at the mining camp below. I did the same, following the path that his eyes took… and what I saw then was something that I'll never forget.

The currents of the river suddenly seemed to race, turned into churning, foaming rapids. The water splashed up against the riverbank, and the watermills began to spin all too quickly, generating shouts of surprise from the workers below. The miners swarmed about, uncertain of what to do.

At that moment, a serpentine creature rose up out of the water. A row of enormous spikes ran down its gleaming sapphire back, and the spikes rippled as it heaved itself out of the water. Its features were shadowed, for it was backlit by the sun, but I could make out a long, fanged snout and two stunning, faceted silver eyes.

Before the miners could react, the magnificent creature reared up out of the river with a mighty surge, lifted its scaly head to the sky… and blinked.

It disappeared so suddenly I thought I would topple from the mountain in shock.

But no matter how invisible it became, it was not gone. With a deafening crash and feathery spray of water, the unseen serpent abruptly dropped itself down onto the riverbank. Watermills shattered, smashed to pieces, and long wooden shafts flew wildly in all directions. Yells sounded as the miners ran about, shielding their faces with their hands.

I was terrified, but something within me forced me to watch. The creature opened its whirling silver eyes and became visible again for the briefest instant. It had lifted its massive bulk up into the skies once more. Its silver eyes stared expressionlessly down at the workers for a long moment, and they cowered with horror in the thing's shadow. I caught a glimpse of scaly, clawed front feet gripping the riverbank; then the creature blinked itself out and sank soundlessly back into the depths.

I stared at Ethan in shock. He was smiling, but his eyes were wide with awe and shock. He seemed almost eager as he looked down upon the miners who were gaping at the wreckage of their watermills.

"What was that thing?" I whispered, hesitant to break the silence.

Ethan turned away and lifted his face to the sun. His smile had vanished. It was a long moment before he replied.

"A river guardian, I think. Some mysteries are not meant to be solved." Then, with slow, almost meandering steps, we walked in silence back down to the new village. We were halfway there before I came to a decision, one that Ethan had been awaiting for a long time.

I reached out and took his arm.

The bright smile he gave me then brought laughter back into my heart, and when we walked into the new village, we were still laughing.

When we shared our news, a group of villagers promptly headed back to check on Charles Charleston's workers. The day after the catastrophe had struck, miners were still milling around the ruined watermills in stunned disbelief.

Eventually, one of the would-be miners began shoving his gear back into his bag, and the others quickly followed his lead, too shocked to do anything else. By noon, they had finished packing up their personal belongings and they quietly left, trickling despondently back between the trees. Notably, none of the miners attempted to use a raft or boat to make their way back down-river.

It might take generations to repair the damage they had done to the riverbank in such a short time, but one thing was clear: the gold would never be theirs.

15. Recovery

The villagers waited and watched from the hills until the last of the miners had dispersed. They would not have to build a new village after all. Delighted and relieved, they happily reclaimed their old cabins, muttering about the mess the miners had left behind.

The mining machines had been abandoned on the south end of the village, hulks of painted iron that would take decades to rust into the ground. Useless to the villagers, they would become a playground for the children and a source of nuts, bolts and other scrap metal to be used for simple tools. In a way, those machines would revolutionize life in the village; despite its short tenure, the intrusion of the mining camp had left a permanent mark.

Always clever with his hands, Ethan was one of the first to pick up on the practical application of the scrap metal. He salvaged a crank and set of blades which made a handy lathe, perfect for carving smooth wooden bowls in a fraction of the time it would take to whittle them. Soon, everyone in the village had a set of his lovely bowls.

Having lived a life of salvage in the city, Runt was quick to teach the other villagers the utility of rubber tires, which could be sliced into long-lasting shoe soles. The soles he made outlasted the shoes themselves, and indeed became family heirlooms, easily reused as the villagers wove new sturdy uppers onto them each season.

Saska, on the other hand, was not so quick to embrace the new technologies of the village. Feeling quite traumatized by the heavy exposure to humans, he disappeared that first night, off into the wilderness where he felt most at home. A gaggle of village children later found the pants and hoodie which he had borrowed strewn along the trail, in various states of disrepair.

Not long afterwards, Uncle John made himself scarce as well. Even Emma, generally a friendly child, stopped making eye contact with anyone but her mother, and she seemed almost sullen. It wasn't long before Estella gave in to Emma's sasquatch heritage and took her out camping, just to get her away from the bustle of village life. Out in the bush, the little girl blossomed.

* * *

They say I'm officially the dreamer for this village, now that the others with this gift have all grown old and passed on. Nana looks at me sternly when she says it, as if to remind me that I can't come and go as I please.

140

For now, I'm just happy to be home. Erin clings to me, as if she would insist on coming with me if I left again. Ethan keeps dropping by with lovely little gifts for us both; carved wooden animals for Erin, berries and other tasty treats for me. He even carved a sinuous, elegant miniature of the river guardian, who now sits on the window sill guarding our cabin. I'm finding myself enjoying the attention for the first time in ages. Ethan has truly taught me to laugh again.

I'm a little afraid of my dreams. What will I do the next time they fill with dire portents? Do I dare settle into the routine of village life, knowing that I could be dragged into the horror of another nightmare?

If my dreams turn dark, can I do anything about it? I felt so helpless to stop the mine's violation of the village, and in the end, it was the river guardian who saved us. There was nothing I could have done to stop the miners from invading.

Perhaps it is time to let go, to take each day as it comes, and to try not to worry too much. It is clear that this land we call home has its own measures of protection.

I just hope that if my help is ever needed again, the land will let me know what to do.

www.ingramcontent.com/pod-product-compliance
Lightning Source LLC
Chambersburg PA
CBHW030533130626
46552CB00006B/2241